Praise for THE JOURNEY HOME:

"I felt the desires of each character, their pains and needs for making it to the place where they were going.... The ending of this book made me feel at peace, content with the way things ended up for everyone in the story. That's a nice feeling to have when you put down a book for the last time."
– My Book Retreat

"Treks the reader through an unforgettable contemporary romance. Hauntingly poignant and beautifully moving, this well-written piece takes the reader on their own journey. This is a touchingly tender story full of emotions that I will definitely recommend to family and friends."
– Coffee Time Romance

"A story that is real and will touch you in many different facets.... An emotional and memorable tale that will stay with you long after the last page. Simply beautiful."
– Minding Spot

"The characters danced in my head and the story jumped off the page and into my soul. *The Journey Home* is a main dish of love, with a side of laughter, a pinch of kindness, and a dash of hope. It left me reliving moments in my life I had long since forgotten about, revealing a love story that I witnessed while growing up, a love story"
– Book Crazy

The Journey Home

Lou Aronica

THE
STORY
PLANT

Studio Digital CT, LLC
P.O. Box 4331
Stamford, CT 06907

Copyright © 2010 by The Fiction Studio

Previously published as Michael Baron.

Story Plant paperback ISBN-13: 978-1-61188-232-2
Fiction Studio Books e-book ISBN-13: 978-1-943486-66-3

Visit our website at: www.thestoryplant.com

First Story Plant Printing: May 2010

For my mother and father.
Your journey inspires me.

Acknowledgements

As always, I want to thank my wife and children for their encouragement, support, and occasional story ideas. Thanks to Baror International and The Story Plant for their energy and commitment. Thanks to Susan Elizabeth Phillips for the great comments and for acknowledging that men can write like this. Thanks to the numerous food magazines, websites, and television shows that have provided me entertainment for so long and have at last become "source material." *Gourmet*, you are gone, but you will never be forgotten. Thanks too to those who have willingly tasted the dishes invented in this novel. Your cast-iron stomachs are an inspiration. Thanks to the Long Island towns that served as models for the places visited in this novel. I never thought I'd ever thank the Long Island Expressway (commonly known as "the world's longest parking lot"), but it too deserves acknowledgment. I'd also like to thank the fans and bloggers who have written such encouraging things about *When You Went Away* and *Crossing the Bridge*. It is exponentially easier to write when people tell you that you've touched them.

The Hearts of Men

What is inside a man's heart? I can't possibly presume to speak for every man, but I can tell you that this question has been a fascination of mine since I was a teenager and I started hearing people say that men weren't in touch with their feelings and that they avoided letting their emotions guide them. That certainly wasn't me, and it certainly wasn't many of the people I knew. Yet this narrative has proven to be a durable one. You see and hear it everywhere – in books, on film, in the media, in coffee shops. I truly believe it is a flawed narrative.

When I began my career as a novelist, I knew that there was only one subject upon which I truly wanted to focus: the hearts of men. I wanted to tell stories from a male perspective that exploded stereotypes and were as honest as I could make them. That has led to this series. You'll meet many men here. Some are just starting their lives, while others have lived it to the fullest. Some are lovers, some are fathers, some are sons. A number of these men have found themselves. Several are still searching. But all of them are facing a moment of dramatic change – a point when who they are and where they are going will be altered forever and when the only way they are going to face up to this change is to explore what's in their hearts.

The third novel in this series is *The Journey Home.* Here, we see two men at very different inflection points in their lives. Joseph wakes up in a place he doesn't recognize around people he doesn't know with a need to get back to his wife, though he doesn't have the slightest idea how to do so. Desperate to get home, he takes to the road. Warren is recently divorced, recently jobless, and currently watching his mother succumb to Alzheimer's. Desperate to find a version of home he can embrace, he follows an unusual path in the hopes of getting there. Both of them will encounter things they couldn't have imagined and change dramatically as a result.

I hope you enjoy *The Journey Home* and its excursion into the hearts of men. I would love to hear your thoughts about it. Feel free to reach out to me at laronica@fictionstudio.com.

ONE - Bring the Sensation Closer

Joseph opened his eyes and nothing seemed familiar. He was lying on a couch – why was he lying down? – in a room he'd never seen before. It was a nice room, a beautiful room, actually, with warm colors and many homey touches, but that wasn't the point. The point was that he'd never seen this room before.

People were looking at him. Four, five, six people in different parts of the room, heads tipped toward him, eyes expressing concern and a hint of curiosity. He sat up quickly and felt light-headed, his vision swimming a bit, until he leaned back against the cushions.

"Where . . ." he said, his voice sounding foreign to him.

A woman perhaps in her late thirties approached him and put a hand on his arm. "Don't exert yourself. You've been through a lot."

Joseph looked at the woman through eyes that were having trouble adjusting to the setting. "Where am I?"

"This is our home," a man with a thick black beard said from off to Joseph's right. "We brought you inside."

"What happened to me?"

The man shrugged and looked at some of the others in the room. "I can't really say."

This was like a bad episode of *The Twilight Zone*. Joseph leaned forward, feeling his head spinning again. When he stood, though, he felt surprisingly strong. Had he passed out on his way to – where had he been going before this happened? He couldn't remember anything.

"Thanks for your help," he said, extending his hand to the man that had last spoken to him. "I'm feeling better now. I should get going."

Another woman, this one seemed to be in her mid-sixties, gestured with both hands for him to sit back down. "Give yourself a little time," she said. "You look a little confused."

Joseph chuckled at that. "Well, yeah, you could say so. I don't normally wake up surrounded by strangers."

"We're safe, if you were worried about that," the first woman said.

It hadn't dawned on Joseph to worry about his safety. He looked at the others in the room. He could tell that they posed no threat. In fact, they seemed pleased to have him around. Maybe they were always dragging people in off the street. Maybe this was just a normal day for them. This didn't seem to have flustered them at all. If someone had passed out in front of his house, he would have been beside himself.

"Dinner's almost ready," the older woman said. "Why don't you have something to eat?"

Now that Joseph thought about it, he was feeling a bit hungry. He couldn't remember the last time he'd eaten. This came as no surprise, since he couldn't remember anything else, either. He tried to call some memory – any memory – to his mind, but it only gave him a headache.

"Thanks. Yeah, that would be good."

While the others in the room moved around, Joseph sat back on the couch, trying to make sense of these incredibly strange circumstances. He looked out the window and saw that the sun was setting. Had he been running errands and gotten into some kind of accident? He tried to remember anything that had happened that day before he woke up here and he couldn't. He truly couldn't remember anything at all. He searched his pockets for clues, but they were empty. Did his hosts steal his wallet and his phone? They didn't seem like the kind of people who would do that sort of thing, but how much did that really mean? Maybe this was all part of their scam. Make him feel that they cared about him, so that he'd never suspect them. Maybe he hadn't passed out; maybe they'd *knocked* him out.

He slumped, rubbing his temples. Closing his eyes, he tried to bring back anything to help him understand what he'd been through today. He didn't feel pain anywhere on his body, so he couldn't have experienced a physical trauma. So much for the people in this room – and it really was just the most comfortable-looking room – assaulting him in some way. However, he had to have been through something extremely traumatic to cause his memory to disappear so completely.

Think, Joseph. Think.

He stared at the nothingness behind his eyelids. Then, from the back of his mind, a sensation crept up slowly. It was sensual and very appealing. It drew him deeper into the couch, relaxing his muscles and soothing his confusion. This sensation had no form and it had no name. But it was definitely human, definitely female, and definitely intimate. Joseph tried to bring the sensation closer, but it eluded him. Whichever way his thoughts moved, the sensation seemed to stay equally far away. Still, he continued to chase it. This meant something, something important. He was certain that if he could find this feeling, his memory would follow.

Slim fingers touched him lightly on the shoulder.

"Dinner is ready, if you'd like to eat," said a feminine voice.

Whatever he'd been trailing disappeared completely. Frustrated, Joseph opened his eyes to see the woman who'd first spoken to him. "Thank you," he said, rising again. His first step felt a bit awkward, but he made it to the dinner table without stumbling.

The first bite of food was surprisingly delicious, and it felt as though he were tasting it with his entire body. Good food did that to him; this much he remembered. The meal was slow-cooked beef that had been simmered in a sauce that had cumin, cinnamon, and tomatoes. It probably meant something that he could pick out all of these flavors, but he couldn't tell what it was. Salt-roasted potatoes and spinach sautéed with garlic completed the plate. Joseph had-n't realized how hungry he was until he started eating. He took several bites before looking up at his table mates, instantly feeling self-conscious about this piggish display of appetite.

"This is great," he said, a little embarrassed. "My compliments to whoever made it."

"That would be Carmela," one man said, gesturing toward a fortyish woman Joseph hadn't noticed before. "We eat like this every night."

Joseph nodded toward Carmela. "Thank you. This is wonderful. If you feed everyone like this every night, they are very, very lucky."

It dawned on Joseph that he had no idea how to define this collection of people. There were six adults of various ages around the table. Some bore a vague resemblance to others, so they could be family. Was-n't it strange for there to be this many adults gathered in one household, though? And no kids? Maybe all of them were out and about.

Carmela thanked Joseph quietly for the compliment. From the soft tone of her voice, he understood why he hadn't noticed her before. Carmela obviously did her speaking through her food. She even seemed to fade into her chair while she was eating.

"I'm Ralph, by the way," said the man sitting next to him, reaching out his hand. "I should have introduced myself earlier."

Joseph put down his fork to shake. "Joseph. I was a little out of sorts earlier, so I probably wouldn't have caught your name even if you'd said it."

"Yeah, I understand. You're looking better now, though. I guess you're getting your legs under you."

Joseph did feel more solid, though he was still completely confused. "A little, I suppose. I'm still trying to figure out what happened. How did you say you found me?"

"I found you," said a woman on the other side of the table who appeared to be in her early thirties. "I'm Maggie. You were unconscious on the sidewalk. I had Ralph and Sal carry you in and put you on the couch."

Unconscious on the sidewalk? The image of a drunk passed out on the curb immediately sprung to mind. That was about as far from Joseph's world as possible, though. Lost memory or not, he was certain about this. He had a glass of wine on occasion, but he hadn't been on a binge since he was a kid.

"This is all very odd," Joseph said, looking down at his plate.

Ralph leaned toward him. "You'll figure it out. You can stay here with us until you do."

Joseph glanced sideways at Ralph and then around the table. They seemed to be waiting for him to respond. Who were these people? They didn't seem strange or predatory to him in any way, but weren't they a little too trusting? After all, even if they weren't dangerous, how did they know that he wasn't dangerous?

"Thanks. That's very kind of you."

Maybe he would stay here tonight. Then, in the morning, he'd try to figure out what was going on. It was entirely possible that a good night's sleep would help bring his memory to him. Then he could head back toward . . .

The sensation that he felt earlier on the couch came back to him. It hadn't retreated as far as he thought it had. It had been there all along, but it had slipped back a little while he was eating and talking to others. For whatever reason, he now knew that this feeling was always there; he felt it the way he felt the air that surrounded him.

My God, she's probably worried out of her mind, Joseph thought as the sensation gained form in his mind. She has no idea what has happened to me – which makes two of us – and she's probably calling everyone she knows. Frustratingly, he couldn't give her a face or a name. He could feel her, but he could-n't touch her. He knew that she was always with him and that she gave him a sense of permanence and support that he could never live without.

He knew that he had to get back to her.

Realizing that the conversation at the table had stopped while he drifted off, Joseph turned toward Ralph again.

"Really, I appreciate it," he said. "If you could put me up tonight, that would be great. I don't think it would be a good idea for me to go out right now. But tomorrow morning I need to get back to my wife."

TWO - Inches from Each Other

"Come join us, Antoinette. You know you love the music."

The nurse had been insisting for minutes now, in spite of Antoinette's quiet, continued refusal. Again, she shook her head no, tightening the collar of her housecoat.

"Jeffrey will be there," the nurse said, teasingly. "You know he's really into you, right?"

Antoinette shuddered at the thought of Jeffrey, or anyone, being "into" her. She was sure Jeffrey was a perfectly pleasant man – she couldn't recall his face right now – but the last thing she wanted was that kind of attention. It was better if she kept her distance from everyone. She wasn't sure what would happen if she tried to get to know someone at this point.

Antoinette still liked her room. Her pictures were here, along with other things she recognized. She didn't like the other side of the door anymore, though. Too many confusing things. Too many things she wasn't sure if she knew. Too many people who were friendly to her but might just be trying to take advantage of her in some way. She had everything she needed right here. The nurses would bring her food after a few minutes of trying to get her to eat in the dining room, and she had all the company she could want right here.

"Maybe tomorrow, Diane," Antoinette said quickly.

The nurse tipped her head to one side. "Now, Antoinette, you know my name is Darlene. And you say 'maybe tomorrow' every day." The nurse moved toward the calendar attached by a magnet to the refrigerator. "Now let me see – yes, it says right here that 'tomorrow' is today!" Darlene or Diane, or whatever her name was today – Antoinette was certain they kept changing it on her – held out her hand. "Come on, Antoinette, we'll dance together. Everyone loves to watch you dance. You're so graceful."

Antoinette stood from the couch and sat on her bed. "Maybe tomorrow. I mean it. I need to rest now."

The nurse let out a huge sigh, her shoulders rising and slumping in exaggerated fashion. "Okay, Antoinette. I'll leave you alone this time. I'm not going to leave you alone tomorrow, though. Ice cream social tomorrow – and I want to see you there eating a *huge* sundae. I'll put the whipped cream on it myself."

She left after that, which made Antoinette feel much, much better. She always felt so much pressure from this nurse. The other one – Jane, Judy, Angela, something like that – was much nicer and much more understanding. For a long time after the nurse left, Antoinette stayed on the edge of the couch, thinking a little about tomorrow's ice cream social and all the people who would be there that she wouldn't recognize, and then not thinking about much. Finally, she stood up, removed her housecoat, and slipped into bed. The sheets hugged her and she warmed to their embrace. As she did, she let her mind drift, knowing it would take her someplace she truly wanted to go.

. . . Today they were walking on a New York City street. Antoinette recognized it as the neighborhood near their first apartment, the place they rented after they married sixty years ago. It was late spring, the sky was clear, and pedestrians bustled around them as Antoinette and her husband walked at their own, very steady, very relaxed pace.

"It's a beautiful day for a walk," she said, "don't you think, Don?"

He took her hand, kissed the back of it lightly, and kept his clasped with hers as they strolled. "It is most definitely a beautiful day, Hannah."

Virtually from the moment they met, they'd called each other "Don" and "Hannah" after the couple played by Fred Astaire and Judy Garland in *Easter Parade*, the movie they saw on their first date. Antoinette was already in love by the time she went out with him for the first time – they'd been flirting for weeks – and when he took her dancing after the movie and called her "Hannah," Antoinette was pretty sure that he felt the same way. From then on, he was her "Don" and she was his "Hannah," and they never used their given names to address each other except on the rare occasion when one of them was very, very angry.

They stopped at a store window so Antoinette could admire a blue chiffon dress. "It's gorgeous, isn't it?"

Don slipped an arm around her waist and put his face close to hers. "It is, and you would look remarkable in it. But I'm afraid it's too expensive."

Antoinette turned to face him, which put their noses inches from each other and made her chuckle. "Too expensive? But we don't even know what it costs."

Don kissed the tip of her nose and then took a couple of steps backward. "I'm afraid I do know what it would cost. You see, the price of the dress itself wouldn't be the issue. The issue has to do with the neckline." He gestured toward the store window. "Do you see how much of your shoulder would be left exposed? As you well know, Hannah, I become senseless with desire around your bare shoulders. That means that, to the price of the dress, we would have to add the fine I would pay for lewd public behavior if you ever wore it out of the house."

He grinned boyishly at that point, and Antoinette shoved him playfully. "That is the worst excuse ever devised to avoid buying me a dress."

"I'm just being practical, darling," he said, still smiling and taking her hand to continue their walk.

They stopped at an electronics store where Don ogled a new radio the way she had ogled the dress. Antoinette tried to come up with an excuse for not buying the radio that was as sappy and romantic as Don's had been for not buying the dress, but her cleverness betrayed her. They left the store without the radio, anyway. In this case, Don really was being practical. They had a comfortable life, but they certainly didn't have the luxury of purely frivolous expenses. The radio in the living room was a perfectly good one, certainly good enough to dance to.

After a cup of coffee and a slice of blueberry pie at Horn & Hardart, they started back toward their apartment. The afternoon had left Antoinette feeling very much at ease. Her muscles felt smooth and her skin warm. Their pace, which had never been rapid, slowed even further, as though they were wading through a pool of the chocolate sauce Don loved for her to make for his ice cream.

Don again raised her hand to his lips and kissed it softly. "I think a nap might be nice when we get home."

She squeezed their hands, which he still held to his face. "Mmm, sounds inviting. Let's stop to get groceries for dinner now so we don't need to go out again later."

"A nap sounds better."

"*Now* it sounds better. When we wake up afterward and you're famished, you'll wish I started dinner."

She turned him toward the market a block from their apartment. She wanted to cook something scandalously rich tonight. A gift for Don. Something to assure him that afternoons like the one they'd just spent were unspeakably precious to her. She chose leeks, cream, and chicken. She remembered noticing that they were low on butter, so she put some of that in her basket as well. Wild rice would be a surprising accompaniment, something that even seemed a little on the naughty side. And the asparagus looked very good.

When they got back to the apartment, Don took to opening the mail while she melted leeks in butter and seasoned the chicken. She was browning the chicken in another skillet when Don came up behind her and wrapped his arms around her waist.

"Smells delicious," he said, kissing the side of her face.

She turned the chicken with a fork. "It's going to taste even better."

He kissed her again. "Do you know what would be even more delicious?"

"What's that?"

"The nap we were talking about."

Antoinette could tell from the feel of him that Don's mind was on anything but napping. "Are you so *sleepy* that you can't wait for me to finish getting this in the oven?"

He kissed her neck now, which left Antoinette feeling as melted as one of the leeks. "I'm very, very sleepy."

"Dinner won't be as good if I leave it now."

"I can live with that," he said, as he began to unbutton the back of her dress and Antoinette began to forget about dinner . . .

The memory faded, but not the sensations that had accompanied the memory. The wonderful, deeply satisfying sensations. Antoinette pulled the sheets up around her neck. Feeling the warmth of his presence in the place she had created for them, she drifted off to sleep. Today had been a very good day.

THREE - *Props*

"Becky told me last night that she was feeling very conflicted about having to choose between us."

Warren got out of the car wearing his Bluetooth earpiece. He hated how people looked when they wore these things in public, but he couldn't get off the phone with Crystal just yet. "Does she realize that the other option would be *not* choosing between us?"

"I mentioned that, but she's taking this very hard. But get this. Do you know what she said? She said if it came down to it, she'd choose you."

Warren's eyes flew open. "She said that?"

"You don't have to sound so elated, you know. You didn't just win the lottery here. And yes, she did say that. If she didn't have the kids and the most perfect husband ever invented, I'd say she was planning to make a move on you."

"Not everything comes down to sexual dynamics, Crystal."

"I'm not saying that everything does. Just most things. We've had that conversation already; many times. The conversation we need to have right now is about the Fidelity fund."

Warren had been walking toward the door of the facility. Now he pivoted to sit on a bench. He didn't want to be in the middle of this conversation in front of his mother or the staff. "I don't understand how this is a negotiating point. I started that fund long before we were married."

"And in the last few years, I've contributed much more to it than you have. Especially in the last year. Have you even put a penny in there recently?"

Warren's eyes narrowed. "We both know why I haven't put any money in there recently. In fact, you even agreed that it was the right decision."

"It *was* the right decision. Especially after you moved out. That doesn't change the fact that I have at least as much right to that account as you have."

Warren's shoulders slackened. "I'm going to be living off of that account soon if I don't find something."

"Then you should find something. Look, I'm willing to compromise. We liquidate the account and each take a share commensurate with the amount we originally invested."

It wasn't that simple, and Crystal knew it. When they had been a team, they apportioned their salaries to different functions. In their flushest years, a chunk of his paycheck went toward the down payment for the bigger house, while a slice of hers went into the Fidelity account for a rainy day. They contributed equally to their retirement account. The rest went into their joint account to pay bills, save for vacations, and for the occasional impulsive expense. It wouldn't be simple, or even appropriate, to sift through this to learn how much of the Fidelity money was his, though he knew if they really did the math, it would turn out that he'd contributed at least eighty percent in one way or another.

"I'm gonna have to sleep on this," he said.

"Don't sleep too long. It's time, Warren."

"You'll get no argument from me there."

"Call me about this tomorrow."

"I will."

Warren ended the call and sat on the bench a minute longer. The sound of Crystal's voice had once energized him. She could literally speed his metabolism just by talking to him. Now any conversation with her left him feeling as though he'd like to lie down for a while. Either that, or huddle in a corner. He felt genuinely weaker sitting here. Every conversation about the divorce sapped him just a little bit more. She was sapping the life force from him, one negotiation at a time. He wasn't even forty yet, but he felt like a hundred and ten.

He took a deep breath and tried to push the enervating details of an unanticipated legal wrangle out of his head. He had to get his spirits up again before going to see his mother.

Treetops Senior Living Center had been her home for the past three years. She'd stayed in the house she shared with Dad, the house in which Warren had been born, for a little more than two years after he died. Her moving here wasn't about her capacities. At seventy-seven, she was still sharp and surprisingly mobile. Rather, it was about her reach. Dad's death had isolated her. Warren couldn't remember a time when his mother and father hadn't seemed utterly integrated into each other's lives, and she seemed baffled over what to do without him, as though she were a car suddenly attempting to drive without an engine. When her next-closest friend Frances moved to Florida, Mom became even less mobile. She left the house infrequently and rarely for more than an hour or so.

It took Warren a few months to convince Mom to look at assisted living facilities with him. She had no interest in going into an "old age home," and she made Warren feel as though he were attempting to put her out to pasture by simply broaching the conversation. She was completely petulant during their first few tours, leaving him feeling guilty even though he knew what he was doing was necessary.

When they visited Treetops, though, she started talking to one of the residents, a woman whose husband had died the year before, and they spent several minutes commiserating. When the woman told Mom that she needed to run because her weekly poker match was starting, Mom watched her walk away as though she desperately wanted to go out to play. She signed the lease the next week, and for the next two years, she seemed revived and social. Warren had a tough time reaching her on the phone because she always seemed to be elsewhere in the complex with her friends.

Then about a year ago, it started to change. She started spending more time in her room. She was sequestering herself again, though this time the outside world was so close to her. Warren had no doubt that he'd find her in her apartment this afternoon. That wasn't the only issue, though. She was closing herself off for a reason, one that Warren struggled to acknowledge. When Mom had allowed loneliness to master her, Warren had a good solution to offer. He had no such solution this time.

Keisha, the boisterous woman at the reception desk, greeted him when he entered.

"Well, aren't you the handsomest thing I've seen all day," she said, handing Warren a visitor's badge.

Warren slipped the nylon-stringed badge over his head. "You're only saying that because I'm the first 'thing' under eighty you've seen all day."

Keisha shook her head in an exaggerated way. "Not true. Not true at all. Mrs. Phelps's grandson was here this morning. Lovely man, but God didn't give him a lot of physical gifts, if you know what I mean. You, on the other hand, are a *specimen.*"

Warren leaned closer to the reception desk. "Keisha, you know if you keep flattering me I'm going to fall in love with you. Then your husband will pummel me, and none of us will come out ahead."

Keisha put a hand to her lips as though she'd been chastened by her transgression. "Too true, Warren. He is a very big and very jealous man." Her eyes sparkled. "You do look very nice today, though."

Warren smiled at the receptionist and then headed down the hallway to his mother's apartment. As he did, he ran into Jan, one of the nurses.

"How's she doing today?" Warren said, nodding in the direction of his mother's room.

Jan tossed her head from side to side, causing her blond bangs to shift back and forth. He guessed that Jan was in her early thirties, though this gesture made her seem a decade younger. "Same as yesterday, really. She almost agreed to come to the ice cream social. I tried to bribe her with extra hot fudge. She didn't go for it, though."

"I can't help but think that shutting herself off makes what's going on in her head that much worse."

"There's no medical reason to think that, but I know what you're saying. She doesn't seem to have much fight."

Warren took a deep breath and looked down the hall. "She's never given in easily before. Even when she was shutting herself off in her house, she still seemed to have a little fight in her."

"Maybe she'll bounce back. I've seen it happen."

Warren's eyes flashed toward Jan's. She didn't withdraw in the slightest, which he appreciated. So many people shrunk away from these conversations, even professionals. "Yeah. Thanks."

Jan touched him lightly on the arm. "I need to go see Mr. Humboldt. Come by after you see her if you want to talk some more."

With that, Jan headed down the hall and Warren continued to his mother's place. He knocked on the door and waited the requisite thirty seconds for her to answer it. When Mom saw it was him, her face opened up and she drew the door wide.

"Warren, honey, how are you? I was just about to make some tea. Would you like some?"

Warren walked into the apartment and kissed his mother's cheek. "Go sit. I'll make it for you."

The apartment came with a two-burner electric stove and a microwave. They were essentially props, since Treetops prepared every meal for the residents, but it made the living space seem more like a home and less like a hotel suite. Warren filled the teapot sitting on the stove with water and put the burner on. Then he sat in a chair next to his mother.

"So, no ice cream for you today?"

Mom's face creased. "I didn't feel like going out today. Maybe tomorrow."

"It's good to get out with your friends. There are a lot of people you like out there."

"I'm good in here."

The teapot whistled a few minutes later and Warren rose to get the tea for them. He opened the cupboard above the stove and found it empty.

"Mom, there's no tea here."

"There must be. I made myself a cup this morning."

On a hunch, Warren looked into the trash for a discarded teabag. As he anticipated, none was there.

"Do you want me to go down to the kitchen to get some teabags?"

"No tea for me, thanks."

Closing his eyes for a second, Warren poured the steaming water into the sink and returned to his seat.

"It's so nice to see you, honey," she said, reaching over to pat him on the knee. Then she pointed to the wall over his right shoulder. "Did you see that I put up that picture of your father and me from the cruise?"

The picture had been up at least six months, his mother having pulled it from the closet filled with pictures she'd had hanging in the house. Warren glanced in that direction and said, "The two of you had a great time on that cruise."

"Your father gained seven pounds on that trip. He would have gained more if I didn't make him take me dancing every night."

"Yeah, that was good thinking on your part."

Mom sat regarding him for a minute, her hands in her lap. "So how's Crystal?"

"I think she's doing fine, Mom. Remember, we're getting a divorce."

Mom's brows knit, as though she were trying to process this information. Then she brightened. "It's so nice to see you, honey. It's the middle of the day, though. Is it okay that you come to visit now? Don't your bosses want you at work?"

Warren grimaced. "They don't want me at work at all, Mom. They let me go a few months ago. That's how I'm able to come here every day."

Mom leaned back on the sofa, her eyelids dropping. "You've told me this before, haven't you?"

This part of the conversation always clutched at Warren's heart. "I have, Mom."

Mom looked down at the arm of the sofa and then at the wall behind Warren. "I'm sorry, honey."

"It's okay, Mom. We can talk about this as many times as you want. It certainly took me long enough to get it through my head."

His mother smiled at him sadly and Warren wished he could take back that last sentence. "Hey, I saw Mrs. Greenwich on the way in. I guess the hip replacement went well because she's looking pretty spry. She tried to pinch my butt, but I managed to sidestep her."

Mom grinned and waved a hand at him. "Don't trust her, honey. She's a man-eater."

"I believe it. Hey, are you sure you don't want to go to the ice cream social? I'll take you. If Mrs. Greenwich tries to make a move on me you can protect me and I'll beat up any of the guys who try to get fresh with you."

"Nah, I'd really rather not. How about a little TV? Ellen is coming on in a few minutes."

Mom reached for the remote and flicked the television to life. Warren sat next to her on the sofa and she looped an arm around his, leaning in his direction. At least he could offer her this comfort. She seemed absorbed in the show immediately.

Watching daytime television had scary implications for Warren. As he glanced down at his mother's placid face, though, juxtaposing it with the expression of consternation she'd shown just minutes before when she realized that he was repeating details for her, he reminded himself that this wasn't about him.

Ellen came dancing through the audience to start her show and Warren shifted his body a little in his mother's direction. A little TV in the afternoon wouldn't hurt.

FOUR - *The First Problem Right There*

Joseph awoke the next morning feeling remarkably refreshed. It was hard for him to believe that he could feel this good only a day after some strangers had found him unconscious on the street. Whatever physical malady had led him to that curb, it hadn't lasted very long. His muscles felt loose and his head felt clear.

Too bad he had no idea where he was or how to get home. Joseph had hoped that a night of sleeping it off would help. He'd even harbored silly, soap-opera fantasies of awakening to discover he'd dreamed the entire thing. That was it; just a trick his mind was playing on him. He'd tell his wife about it when he got up and they'd spend all of breakfast trying to figure out what it meant.

When he got out of bed, though, he found Carmela baking cinnamon rolls in the kitchen, and Ralph, Sal, Maggie, and the others drinking coffee. This was most definitely not a dream, though it was still impossible for him to believe it was real. He also found that his memory had not improved in any way that mattered. The "feel" of his wife was still there, but her identity and location continued to elude him. Everything else was even weaker than that. He had no idea of his last name, what he did for a living, whether or not he had kids, friends, a dog, or even if he lived in the city or the suburbs. Strangely, he knew that all of these things existed in the world, but he couldn't identify anything more specifically. It was as though he'd been plopped down in a foreign land with the kind of training that came from a book, but not a single bit of practical knowledge.

The people around the table convinced him to stay for breakfast. He was thankful he did. Carmela's baking was as accomplished as her cooking. However, he told them he had to get on the road home immediately thereafter. He mentioned that he was going to check to see if anyone had filed a missing person's report yesterday. Though Joseph couldn't even give his last name, he thought he'd at least get a clue from this. However, Ralph told him that he'd already called the police department that morning and Joseph had not been reported missing.

Joseph sipped a second cup of coffee and listened to the others discussing their plans for the day. Then, thanking them profusely for their help and their hospitality, he left the house.

It was only at that point that he fully acknowledged that he had no plan. It was possible that one of the cars on the street was his – he could have gotten this far, left the car, and then passed out; it was an explanation as good as any other – but he couldn't say which. He didn't have keys in his pocket, anyway, so even if he had a car, he wouldn't be able to drive it. Reaching into his pockets now, he confirmed that his wallet and phone were still gone. However, he pulled out a surprisingly large wad of cash. Had he made a huge withdrawal from the bank before his episode? If that were the case, why wouldn't whoever took his other things have taken the money as well? If he'd been mugged, the mugger wasn't particularly good at his job. This story just kept getting stranger and more elusive.

Joseph counted out the cash, a significant sum, and then glanced up and down the road. What was the next move here? Was there a bus or train station nearby? What would he say to the person selling him the ticket? "Home, please?"

Putting the money in his pocket, he stood stock-still, unsure where even his first step should take him.

"You look a little lost."

Joseph turned toward the voice to his right. A teen-aged boy was standing perhaps ten feet away, hands in his pockets. He was lanky, close to six feet, with a mess of black hair coming at his face from a variety of angles. His eyes were a radiant blue.

"Why do you say that?" Joseph said.

"People don't usually just stand here on the street. Most people have somewhere to go. Since you didn't, I guessed you were lost."

There was a bit of wryness in the boy's tone, but it didn't seem sarcastic. Amused, perhaps, but not sarcastic.

"I think it's fair to say that I'm lost. Let me put it this way: I'm so lost that I don't even know if I'm lost."

"That doesn't sound good. Where are you trying to go?"

"There's the first problem right there."

The kid looked down at the pavement and then back up at Joseph, wearing an expression that said that Joseph had just told him one of the most ridiculous things he'd ever heard. "I'd say you were *very* lost."

Joseph slumped. "Yeah, me too."

The kid shook his head compassionately, which Joseph's guidebook training told him was somewhat unusual for a teen. Feeling surprisingly comfortable with yet another new stranger, Joseph told the boy about everything that had happened in the past day, including the certainty he felt about his wife being out there some-where, waiting for him, worrying about him. Simply saying these things aloud made the feelings stronger for Joseph. The pull he felt in the back of his head intensified as he spoke.

The boy cast him a sidelong glance. "But you have no idea where you live."

"None."

"You know you have to get back there, though."

"That's the one thing I'm completely sure about."

The kid looked off for a second and then regarded Joseph with new resolve in his eyes. "I'll go with you."

"What?"

"I've been telling myself for weeks that it's time for me to get out of here. I always find a reason to hang around, though. I think you're my sign that it's really time to go."

Joseph looked at the boy skeptically. Was the kid messing with him, trying to have some fun at the expense of a confused guy he met on the street? "How old are you?"

"I'm seventeen."

"That would mean you aren't technically able to simply go with me."

The kid shrugged and tossed his hair "Depends on what you mean by 'technically able.' I guess I'm officially a minor, but I don't think anyone would give me a hard time about that."

"Like your parents?"

The kid's eyes softened a bit. "I lost my parents when I was a little kid. I've been living with these people. They're very nice, but, you know . . ."

Joseph gave the boy an opportunity to explain further, but the kid didn't say anything more. Instead, he just looked at Joseph, as if he were appraising him, or testing him.

Finally, Joseph broke the silence. "Amazingly, taking you along with me wouldn't even be the strangest thing that's happened to me in the past day. A couple of little problems, though: I have no idea where I'm going, and I have no way of getting there."

"I can help you with the second part." The boy pointed to a blue Camry across the street. "That's mine. You pay for the gas."

Joseph stared at the car for what must have been close to a minute. Then he turned to the boy and said, "This doesn't seem ridiculous to you?"

The boy offered a lopsided grin. "Yeah, of course it does. But you need to get somewhere." His brows furrowed. "And so do I."

Joseph looked at the car, then at the sky, and finally at the kid. "Then let's go."

They walked across the street – had a single car even passed while they had been standing there? – and entered on their respective sides. The kid put his key in the ignition and then offered his hand to Joseph.

"I'm Will, by the way."

Joseph took the hand. He hadn't expected the kid to have such a strong grip. "Joseph."

Will started the car and checked the mirrors. He obviously hadn't been driving very long because he took every precaution before he put the car in gear. "Do you want to pick a direction?"

Joseph closed his eyes and tried to feel for his wife. As always, the sensation was there, though it didn't take any palpable form. He opened his eyes and pointed at a thirty-degree angle from where the car was parked. "That way."

"That way it is," Will said, moving out of his parking spot.

"I'm hoping I can be a little more specific as we get farther along."

"That would be good. At least we're heading somewhere, though."

Yes, Joseph thought, at least we're heading somewhere.

FIVE - Like Crazy

Antoinette settled into the bed, hugging her pillow closer to her as she did so.

. . . She jumped from the couch when the door-bell rang.

"Is that Mr. Dreamboat?" her mother called from the kitchen.

"Mother, you promised that you'd never use that name in front of him. You still promise, right?"

"Of course, dear."

Antoinette opened the door, grinning. She planned to assault Don with kisses. However, when she saw the tight expression on his face, she simply held the door to usher him into the living room. They sat on the couch and Don finally leaned over to kiss her. In the six months that they'd been dating, she couldn't ever remember their first kiss of the night taking that long. He usually kissed her before he even said a word. Of course, he hadn't actually said a word yet tonight, either.

"You seem a little . . . scary," Antoinette said tentatively. "What's wrong?"

Don let some of the tension go out of his body and put his hand in hers. His eyes softened, too; he no longer looked like he was on a hunt.

"I'm sorry, Hannah I didn't mean to scare you. I'm a little tense, that's all."

"Can I help you with anything?"

"Not unless you have a spare father lying around."

Don's lips pulled together and his color deepened. "I had

dinner with him tonight. He said he wanted to have a 'man-to-man' with me. What he really wanted to do was have a 'man-to-useless-waste-of-a-person' with me. He spent the entire time telling me how much of a disappointment I was to him."

Antoinette squeezed Don's hand. "He said that to you?"

"Not in those words, exactly. Actually, what he said was worse. He told me that he thought I'd been making terrible decisions since I was a teenager. He said I was throwing away my time on unrealistic expectations for my career, and that if I didn't learn a trade soon, I'd wind up a beggar on the street."

"He didn't actually say *that*, did he?"

"You're right; he didn't say, 'beggar.' I think the word he used was 'bum.' Yes, 'bum,' that was definitely it."

"Oh, Don."

Don had barely spoken about his father in the half year Antoinette had been with him. She had met his parents on a few occasions, but she and Don never spent time there. Antoinette had always assumed that they visited at her house because her mother was always baking for him and fawning over him – she could smell brownies in the oven right now, as a matter of fact. From what Don was telling her as they were sitting here, though, that wasn't the reason at all.

"He thinks I don't have the talent to be an executive, in spite of how well things are going for me at the company. He thinks they're going to find out soon enough that I'm just a dope and then they'll kick me out the door."

"Your boss told you just the other day that you're one of the sharpest trainees they've ever had. They've been complimenting you left and right. Did you tell your father that?"

Don stood anxiously. She'd never seen him struggle like this to contain himself. He'd always been so cool.

"He even managed to turn that against me. He told me that corporations use those techniques to squeeze everything they can out of trainees before they toss them aside. How would he even know that? He's a pipe fitter!" Antoinette reached a hand for Don to try to bring him back to her. She'd never seen him in so much pain and she wanted to hold him and let him know that she believed in him. She supposed it was possible that Don's father knew something about how corporations worked, but that didn't mean he was right about Don. Any corporation would know how lucky they were to have him and they would do everything they could to keep him.

Just then, her mother came into the living room with the brownies on a tray with two glasses of milk. Antoinette was afraid that Don might say something sharp because he was so tense, but he greeted Mother warmly, even complimenting her housedress, which always set Mother fluttering. Antoinette signaled with her eyebrows that her mother should leave them alone, and fortunately she did so. Mother probably thought they wanted to snuggle. Little did she know that Antoinette was having trouble getting Don to even stop pacing around the room.

When she was gone, Don returned to the couch and Antoinette circled him with her arms, feeling him ever so gradually relax. They didn't say anything for several minutes. This felt okay, though. This felt natural. This was who she wanted to be for Don. She wanted to be someone he could always count on. She wanted to be his safe place.

Eventually, Don looked up at her, his expression wistful now, and said, "I swear, Hannah, I will never treat our children that way."

The words took Antoinette so completely by surprise that she literally gulped. It wasn't the most graceful sound in the world. "Our children?"

Don shut his eyes tight and held that pose for something like fifteen seconds. When he opened them at last, he seemed embarrassed, but his eyes gleamed. He turned to face her. "That is definitely not how I intended to do this."

Antoinette's stomach started to clench. "Do what, Don?"

"Talk to you about . . . our future."

Antoinette found that she couldn't speak. Of course, she thought about her future with Don all the time. She knew he loved her and she couldn't imagine anything pulling them apart. Still, the idea of addressing that future, right now, when only minutes before Don had seemed so shaken, left her speechless. All she could do was nod her head slowly, though even that took effort because she was so nervous.

"Hannah, you're everything in the world to me. I've looked at you that way since our very first dance. Whatever my father makes me feel, you make me feel the opposite. I feel like a king with you. I feel – "

" – Exactly the way you should feel. I believe in you completely, Don."

Don's eyes glistened and he looked at her as though she were the most beautiful thing in the world. Nothing was better than that look.

"I love you like crazy, Hannah."

He squeezed her hand, which Antoinette hadn't even noticed he was holding until now. "I love *you* like crazy, Don."

He patted one pocket with his free hand, and then the other, looking down as though he thought he might find something there. "I'm not prepared for this. I was thinking maybe Christmas, or your birthday or something." Suddenly, his eyes flashed up to hers and he took both of her hands into his lap. "I can't wait, Hannah, and I know

I'm making a mess of this. But I'm not going to stop now that we've started." He brought her hands to his face and kissed each gently, his lips just barely brushing them. His combination of strength and gentleness was an endless revelation. Antoinette thought it was entirely possible that she was going to swoon, though she very much wanted to stay awake for this moment.

"Hannah, will you marry me?"

Antoinette leaped into Don's arms with such force that they toppled onto the floor, crashing into the coffee table and sending brownies in every direction. She didn't care about the mess; you could clean up a mess in a few minutes. She only cared about showing Don the joy he always brought to her heart – especially now.

"Is everything okay up there?" Mother yelled out. She'd gone down to the den to watch television with Father.

"Everything is great, Mother," Antoinette said, hoping her mother wouldn't come up the stairs to confirm this.

She kissed Don and then got up from the floor, smoothing her skirt as she did so. Staying on the floor with him right then would have been far preferable, but not with her parents so nearby.

She settled back on the sofa and Don sat next to her, holding her hands. He was beaming and Antoinette knew she was smiling at least as broadly. "Should we go tell them now?"

"I don't have a ring. I really wasn't planning this tonight. And to think I was in a lousy mood when I came here."

"I'm not sure how long I'll be able to keep this inside of me."

Don held up a finger. "One more day. I know exactly what ring I want to buy you. I'll get it tomorrow and we'll make this official."

Antoinette tipped her head sideways. "Are you saying it isn't official now?"

Don smiled. "I'm not getting anything right tonight, am I? It is definitely official, my dear Hannah. As official as the rest of our lives."

With that, they were toppling off the sofa again. Mother was going to come up; she was sure of it . . .

The knock at the door startled Antoinette out of her reverie. She stayed in bed with her eyes closed and fingers twirling her engagement ring, hoping whoever was knocking would go away. The knock came again, this time more insistent. Why couldn't people leave her alone? Why couldn't they simply accept that she was where she wanted to be?

When the knock came a third time, Antoinette pulled her body out of her bed, put on her housecoat, and made her way on sagging legs to the door. Still angry, she pulled the door open with as much force as she could muster and scowled at the intruder.

"Mom, are you okay? You look like your head's about to explode."

SIX - Enmeshed in the Details

Mom turned and headed toward the couch as deliberately as her varicose-veined legs would carry her.

"I'm fine, I'm fine," she said, sitting heavily and twirling her engagement ring around on her finger.

Warren closed the apartment door and then sat across from her. "You don't look fine, Mom. Did someone do something to get you angry? Did *I* do something to get you angry?"

Mom continued to watch the twirling ring for several additional seconds. When she finally looked up, she seemed more melancholy than angry. "Your father asked me to marry him."

"Well, yeah, I kind of assumed that. Isn't that the way it usually was back when you two were dating? I guess you could have asked him, but didn't that kind of thing create a scandal?"

Anger seemed to flare up in Mom's eyes again for a moment, but it dissipated quickly, replaced by consternation. "That's not . . . never . . . never mind."

Warren had no idea what his mother was trying to say to him. He knew his inability to understand her frustrated her, but when he'd tried to explore these conversations further in the past, he'd only managed to upset her more. The anger concerned him, though. Given the vast amount of spare time he had these days, he'd been doing some reading, both books and online, about what he was seeing in her condition. He knew it was possible that her rage might become a common thing, and he wasn't sure how well he'd be able to handle that. He couldn't think of a single time when his mother had gone off on him, even when he'd done incredibly stupid things as a kid. His friends regularly complained about enduring lectures and tongue-lashings. He'd never had to deal with that, and he appreciated it.

Her face had become more placid now, almost as though she were using some kind of stress-relief technique. Warren had attempted to get her to try meditation a few years ago, having heard that it could help with mental acuity, but she wouldn't even consider it. Whatever she was doing now was certainly relaxing her, though. Maybe Jan or one of the other nurses had taught it to her. It seemed to take years from her.

"He's worried that he fumbled it. He doesn't have a ring. I don't care about a ring – at least right now. I just wanted him to ask me."

Mom's talking about Dad was hardly new. A good third of every conversation they'd had since Dad died had centered on him in some way. Stories about their courtship, about their early married days, about the adventures they had after Warren moved out of the house, which always made him feel a little jealous even though he'd moved on to his own adventures. The difference here was that she was talking about this event as though it had just happened, as though she were telling a girlfriend about it on the phone.

This was a new wrinkle, and one with which Warren had some trouble contending. Did he engage her in this talk, pretending that they'd transported sixty years into the past (in which case, did he need to identify who she thought he was in this scenario)? Did he attempt to snap her out of it, which might be harmful on a number of levels? Did he simply sit here and let her keep talking, assuming that she'd step out of the past at some point? This last option was becoming more attractive as the moments passed.

Warren had never known his parents when they were in the blush of adulthood. They were in their early forties when they had him, having already been married for more than twenty years. There were photographs and reminiscences, of course, and these gave this period some semblance of substance for Warren. In the five years since Dad died, Mom had painted in the background even more, giving voice to the great joys and deep heartaches of those years with the enthusiasm of a professional biographer. She'd become so enmeshed in the details of a story that Warren sometimes thought he could put on his shoes, take a quick stroll through the neighborhood, chat up the guy that lived next door for a while, and come back to find his mother still recounting the same tale. He never wanted to do anything of the sort, though. The stories gave form to his family history. They answered questions he didn't realize he should have asked. They made the long past that existed before he entered their world come alive for him.

He missed it when his mother's recounting became far less voluble. It should have been a sign to him that something was happening to her mind when her storytelling became less florid. If he'd noticed it faster, could the doctors have been more effective in stemming her decline? The drugs they were trying now showed no impact, but they might have been more effective if physicians had started the treatment earlier.

The silence had extended for several minutes now. Warren had stopped watching his mother as he drifted into his own thoughts. When he looked at her now, though, he saw that she was staring behind him. At first, he thought she was looking at the photograph on the wall, but then he remembered that the picture was over his other shoulder. He turned to see what had captured her attention, but found nothing there.

When he turned back, her eyes were locked on his. This startled him, as though he hadn't realized she was in the room with him, and he flinched. The motion seemed to generate some spark within his mother and the scowl with which she greeted him returned.

Then, just as quickly, it fell. This time, though, she didn't seem to relax. Instead, she seemed to sag. Without a word, she stood, patted him gently on the cheek, and walked away from him. As Warren watched, she removed her housecoat, climbed into bed, and pulled the sheets around her.

Was that it? Was that the extent of their visit for the day? Should he leave? If he did, would she even remember that he'd been there?

For the second time in the last fifteen minutes, Warren felt stuck. Leaving seemed wrong, but staying seemed silly. He was still pondering this when he heard a knock at the door. Faced with an easy decision at last, he opened it to find Jan on the other side.

"Hey," she said as she entered the room. "I need to check Antoinette's blood pressure."

"Checking her blood pressure requires touching her, right?"

Jan wrinkled her nose. "That or Vulcan mind meld."

"Yeah, you might want to go with the latter."

Jan put down the supplies she'd carried into the room. "Problem?"

Warren plopped onto the couch where his mother had sat only minutes earlier. "She's been a little unpredictable since I got here. If you try to take her blood pressure, she might be as cooperative as usual. Or she might have your left hand for a snack."

Jan sat on the arm of the chair across from him, exhibiting more concern than he would have liked her to exhibit at that moment. "Where is she?"

"She went back to bed a few minutes ago. I assume she's sleeping, because I haven't heard her move."

"And you're staying here?"

Warren chuckled softly and looked upward toward Jan's eyes. "Pretend that you aren't thinking that I have absolutely nothing else to do with my life, okay?"

"What I was thinking was that you were the world's greatest son." Jan slid into the chair. She was wearing a blue, knee-length skirt and Warren couldn't help but notice her calves as she sat.

"Sitting here while she sleeps is nothing. Watching game shows with her for two hours? That's true selflessness."

"Or a case of having nothing else to do with your life."

Warren was surprised that Jan would tease him this way. Of course, he'd essentially invited her to do so. "Or that," he said, grinning.

Jan tossed her head in the direction of his mother's room. "She's having mood swings?"

"Today her mood was all over the place. There haven't been many days like this. Yet."

Jan touched her fingertips together. "We should probably get some more tests."

"Isn't that a little bit like testing the ocean for wetness?"

Jan pressed her lips together, then brought her steepled fingers to her mouth. "Do you think this is rattling her?"

Warren leaned into the sofa, rubbing his left temple. "Less and less, I think. Which of course means it's rattling me more and more."

Jan leaned toward him, and for a moment Warren thought she was going to hug him. Instead, she just looked at him for a long beat. This had the potential to become uncomfortable, but before they reached that point, Jan put her hands on her knees, which he also couldn't help noticing, and stood from the chair.

"I'm going to have to take my chances and get that blood pressure reading."

"Can I have you sign a waiver first?"

"The facility has us covered." She took a step toward Mom's bedroom and then turned back to him. "We can talk about this anytime you want, you know. Unfortunately, I have quite a bit of experience with it."

"Thanks. I'm going to take you up on that."

Jan started moving toward the bedroom again. "That's good."

Warren watched Jan go through the doorway and listened to her gentle voice as she coaxed his mother into offering up her arm. A minute later, she was waving good-bye to him.

Alone, and with far more time on his hands than he should have, Warren turned on the Game Show Network.

SEVEN - *Somewhat More Palpable*

Three hours of highway driving had done nothing to bring a sense of direction to Joseph's journey. The names of towns they passed had varying levels of familiarity, but Joseph didn't know if this had something to do with his knowledge of the area, or with the generic sound of the names. Did every state in America have a Springfield? Had he actually spent time in Green Valley, Riverbend, or Hillsdale, or were the names just variations on Anywhere USA? Certainly, none of them inspired him to suggest that Will exit for a closer look.

The boy had been an entertaining traveling companion, though his references to sports and popular culture proved frustrating. None of the names meant anything to Joseph. He recognized some of the cities, not enough to identify with any of them, but enough to know that he'd heard of them before. He had a feeling that he'd been an avid baseball fan, but at gunpoint, he wouldn't have been able to name the team that played in Chicago. It was as though his memory were playing an elaborate game of peek-a-boo with him, revealing part of itself for an instant before hiding away again.

Will turned up the car stereo to play a song that he seemed to enjoy. He had varied taste in music, some of which sounded better to Joseph than others. Music seemed to be something of a passion for the boy, and he moved while he drove, with as much grace as a seat belt and a steering wheel afforded. This latest tune had him playing bass guitar with the turn signal while he rocked his head in syncopation. Joseph grinned at the sight, and even found his right foot moving to the song's insistent rhythm. When the music ended, Will turned down the volume before the next song began.

"Was that a great cut or what?"

"I liked it. It was one of the better ones you've played. Who was that performer?"

"Vampire Weekend." Joseph arched his eyebrows. "The band's name is really Vampire Weekend?"

Will threw up his hands. "Hey, I don't name 'em; I just love 'em."

Joseph chuckled at the boy's enthusiasm. He was a fascinating combination of cool and childish.

"You'll let me know if you're getting tired, right?"

"I'm good."

"Are you sure? We've been driving for a while now."

Will glanced over at him with the lopsided grin that Joseph had quickly recognized as his signature. He guessed that girls recognized it as something else. "Are you telling me that *you're* tired?"

"I wouldn't mind stretching my legs for a little while."

"Next rest stop we come to, okay?"

About fifteen minutes later, Will turned off the highway and up a long ramp to a stop marked "Frank Capra Memorial Rest Stop." The name Frank Capra only rang the dimmest of bells in Joseph's mind, but the rest stop dedicated to him had a remarkable folksy quality. They passed gas pumps on their way off the ramp, but the vicinity around the rest stop was like the main street of a very small town. Trees lined the curb and patrons milled from an ice cream shop to a dry goods store to a restaurant bearing a sign that promised homestyle cooking, the best coffee for miles, and "Bethy's incomparable pies."

"Are you hungry?" Joseph said to Will as they got out of the car.

"I could eat something."

"Let's go see what this 'homestyle cooking' is about."

They entered a room with soft lighting and muted colors. Perhaps this was just further evidence of his failed memory, but Joseph had not envisioned this when he imagined going to a rest stop. The tables and chairs were maple with woven, amber-colored placemats at each setting. Moss green drapes hung from the windows, matching the moss and beige rug on the floor. If the cooking was as "homestyle" as the dining room decor, this meal was going to be far more of a treat than Joseph had expected. That would be good. The only time he'd felt truly comfortable since awakening in this place had been when he was eating, but he also hadn't had a thoughtless meal yet.

The hostess seated them and handed them menus. A busboy brought them water as they sat and a waiter took Joseph's order for coffee and Will's for a Sprite. Joseph opened his menu and considered the options. Four-cheese pasta sounded appealing, as did the chicken-and-white-bean chili. A box on the righthand corner of the menu told the story of "Randy's famous spice-rubbed smoked pork loin," explaining how Randy (whoever he was) had spent years experimenting with spices, woodsmoke, and cooking temperatures before perfecting this dish.

"Hey, did you see this thing about the pork?" Joseph said to Will, who'd already closed his menu.

"Nah, I didn't notice it."

"It sounds very impressive. I think I hear it calling to me."

Will looked down at the menu, but didn't reopen it. "A turkey sandwich works for me."

Joseph screwed his face into an expression of disbelief. "Really? With all the other interesting stuff they have here?"

Will shrugged. "Food's not that big a deal to me."

Joseph found that sentiment baffling. How could food not be a big deal? *Everybody* loved food, didn't they? He could imagine this becoming a problem between the two of them if they stayed on the road for any length of time. Joseph decided right then that he'd take charge of every one of their meals while they were traveling. Life was far too short to eat badly.

Joseph ordered his smoked pork and Will his turkey sandwich, and the waiter promised to get their meals out to them as quickly as he could. When the waiter left, Will took a sip of his drink and then leaned toward Joseph.

"Okay, tell me everything about her."

"About who?"

"Your wife."

Joseph lowered his eyes. "You know as much about her as I do."

Will became more animated. "No, I don't. You know *tons* about her. Dig down and pull something out."

Joseph had no idea what the kid was getting at. Did Will think that Joseph had been holding out on him, that he'd been spinning some elaborate yarn about losing his memory? He threw an accusing glance across the table, but what came back at him wasn't provocation. It was encouragement. Will was trying to goad him into figuring things out. The kid had some surprises in him. *Dig down?* Okay, he'd try. Staring at his lap, Joseph tried to get his mind to cooperate with his desires. She was in there somewhere. Did he have the strength to bring her out? He closed his eyes and tried to reach out for the wisp of her he knew was always there. As he did, she became somewhat more palpable. Flexing open his right hand, he felt the satin of her upper arm. The warmth and smoothness, colored by a tiny mole. The subtle contour of her upper bicep. The curve of her perfect shoulder that led to her long, regal neck whose skin was almost impossibly smoother. He parted his lips slightly and felt hers. The way they yielded to and at the same time embraced his had been a breakthrough for him the first time they kissed. Before this, he had never known that a kiss could be both pillowy and firm. It drew him to a need to kiss her that extended far beyond attraction and passion. It was as though he had discovered something necessary to his welfare, some secret thing that allowed him to live his life at a higher and now completely essential level. His chest warmed and he could feel her skin on his, molded with his as they lay in the night. Joseph knew he'd be able to sense her heartbeat if he were still enough, if he let himself melt into her. Yes, there it was, issuing its subtle throb into his own pulse. Joseph sank into the rhythm of it. This was something absolutely, uniquely hers. It bore her essence. It would take him to her. But while he continued to feel her heartbeat, his journey toward his wife ended right there. He implored his mind to go deeper, to go beyond touch, to offer the same fullness of experience to his other senses. As he did so, though, the throbbing of her heart lessened. His skin grew cooler. His lips and his fingers touched nothing but air. He opened his eyes and looked across at Will, who stared back at him as though waiting for the next detail in an incredibly enticing story.

"You had something there," the boy said. "Didn't you?"

"No."

"Nothing?"

"Not enough."

Will slumped, as though someone had let the air out of him. "It sure seemed like something was going on."

Joseph shook his head slowly. "Something. Just not anything that makes where we're trying to go clearer."

Will ran a hand through his hair. "That sucks. You got my hopes up for a second there."

"Sorry to let you down."

The waiter came with their plates. Joseph's meal was fragrant with smoke and sage. He could smell the care that went into this dish and he wanted to enjoy it. He wondered if he could muster enthusiasm for it, though. The retreat of his wife's touch had blunted his appetite for anything else.

EIGHT - *Aromatics*

Still feeling doubtful about the entire thing, Antoinette opened the closet door and put on the winter coat she saw there. Warren had said that all the things in this closet were hers, so she picked out the one that looked nicest.

"Mom, it's seventy degrees out," Warren said, walking up to her and helping her to remove the coat. "I just thought you might want a sweater or something." He hung the coat in the closet and pulled out a thin jacket. "This'll be good," he said, as he held it up for her to put on.

He was insisting on taking her out, saying it would be good for her, even though she protested strongly that she didn't want to go. Antoinette doubted it would be good for her – there was only one good place for her now – but she agreed to do so because she was sure Warren would just keep nagging her until she did. It was good for *him*, maybe. He was probably just bored of being with her and wanted to get out, and he figured he had to lug her around if he were going to do so. He could have just gone to lunch by himself if he was so antsy. She didn't need him to be here if he didn't want to be here.

When they left the apartment, they passed several people in the hallway, some of whom said hello to her. Antoinette didn't recognize any of them, but she smiled and nodded. The nurse that was usually nice to her came up to them and said something about Antoinette's going on an "excursion." Then she said something to Warren that Antoinette couldn't hear. The nurse seemed a little too familiar in her attitude toward Warren. Antoinette would have to remind her that her son was married. She never appreciated a woman who tried to put herself between a man and his wife.

Antoinette felt the breeze the second they walked out the door. Warren had an arm looped around one of hers, but she used her free hand to cinch the jacket around her neck. The heavier coat would have been better. She should have just trusted her own mind.

"The car's right over here," Warren said, moving her toward the back end of the parking lot. If he knew he was going to drag her out of her apartment today, he should have parked closer. This was just another indication that he was doing this for himself and not for her.

They drove down a street lined with trees that had white blossoms on them, and then turned onto a busy road. The cars drove very fast around here, not like where she and Don lived. And so many stores. Who bought all those things?

"Are you hungry, Mom?" Warren said as he tried to keep up with the other cars. "I thought we could go to that diner you always liked."

"That would be fine." Antoinette wasn't very hungry and she had no idea which diner her son was talking about, but she didn't want to get into a conversation with him right now. He needed to concentrate on the road. Two hands on the steering wheel would be nice, also.

"Do you need anything while we're out?"

"No, I don't think so."

"Are you sure? We can go to the mall after we eat, if you'd like."

"That's okay. They give me everything I need, really."

Warren stopped at a traffic light and gestured around them. "They're doing a ton of building all over here.

They're putting in a huge new Target down the block.
You'll have a field day in there when it's open. Can you
believe how much this area is changing?"
Warren seemed excited about all the new stuff. Antoinette would have to take his word for it. She looked out
the window and tried to get her bearings, but then the car
was moving again and she lost her place.

A few minutes later, Warren pulled his car into a parking lot. Antoinette assumed they'd arrived at the diner
he'd been talking about. He came around to her side of
the car and helped her out, which Antoinette appreciated
since her legs had tightened up during the drive. Holding
on to her son's arm, she carefully climbed the five steps
up to the diner's entrance.

The place seemed pleasant enough. There were mirrors on the wall, which gave Antoinette multiple reflec-
tions of herself. She should have done something with
her hair, and would have if Warren had given her more
warning. A large case to the right of the front door was
full of oversized baked goods. The cakes seemed ridiculously high. Did people actually eat those things?

A hostess welcomed them and sat them in a booth
in the large dining room. Everything here seemed to be
some shade of brown. It wasn't particularly unpleasant,
and it seemed clean, but a little color would have helped
immensely. Don used to laugh at her about her penchant
for splashing color all over their house, especially in the
dining room and the kitchen. She always reminded him
that people ate with their eyes as much as their stomachs,
and he always responded by telling her that her cooking
was so good that he could have feasted blindfolded. She
loved when he cut off any disagreement with a compliment. He always knew what to say.

Antoinette looked at her menu for a few minutes
before deciding to have a couple of scrambled eggs and

toast. It had been a long time since she'd felt any kind of appetite. She probably would have been fine with just some coffee, but Warren would have been disappointed. He even questioned her about choosing eggs before he ordered a cup of soup and a chicken potpie. She didn't want to let him down – he seemed excited about bringing her here – but the eggs were going to be enough of a challenge.

"Is your soup okay?" Antoinette said when the cup arrived a few minutes later.

"Yeah, yeah, it's fine." Her son held his spoon toward her. "Do you want to try?"

Antoinette waved a hand. "No, thanks."

Warren spooned a noodle and some broth, then sipped. "You're not missing anything. Not exactly your home cooking, Mom."

"Restaurant food is different."

He reached for the pepper and shook it over his cup several times. "It's definitely different. But why eat at home when you can pay so much more for something that doesn't taste nearly as good?"

Antoinette reached out to pat her son's arm. He was a good boy. "You always appreciated my cooking."

"The whole neighborhood appreciated your cooking. Did you ever notice how many of my friends showed up just before dinnertime?" He took another spoonful of soup and wrinkled his nose. "Mrs. Feinberg cooked like this. That's why Paul was always hanging out at our house."

Antoinette dipped her spoon in the cup and tasted. Warren was exaggerating about how bad the soup was, but only by a little. "Too much salt," she said. "And much too much pepper, though that might not have been *their* fault. More aromatics in the broth would have helped."

Warren smiled at her as though she'd just revealed a gigantic secret. "I'm telling you, Mom, you should have opened that restaurant we always talked about."

"*You* always talked about it, not me. I never liked the idea of cooking for strangers. I didn't even like cooking when your father brought home people from work. Cooking is for family."

"I'm telling you, Mom, all of the customers would have thought you were cooking just for them. You could have scored big."

She looked out at him over arched eyebrows. "And who says that I didn't score big?"

Warren gave her a quick bow with his head. "Fair enough."

Antoinette's plate came at that point and she tasted her eggs. At least she thought she tasted them. She couldn't be certain because they didn't seem to have any flavor.

"Honey, could you pass me the pepper? You'd better give me the salt, too."

He handed both shakers across the table. "That yummy, huh?"

"Just like home." She grinned. "At least, just like Paul Feinberg's home."

Warren laughed like Antoinette had just told the funniest joke in the world. She liked that she could get that kind of reaction from him. Maybe letting him get out with her wasn't such a bad idea after all.

Warren seemed to like his potpie a little more than he liked his soup, and Antoinette seasoned her eggs further in an attempt to coax some flavor out of them. You had to *try* to make eggs taste this bland. Since she wasn't particularly hungry anyway, though, she gave up after a few bites. When Warren finished his lunch, they ordered coffee and chatted. Antoinette asked her son about his wife and his job, which seemed to fluster him for some reason. She wondered what was going on. It wasn't like him to be so closemouthed. Warren had always been very willing to talk to her about what was going on in his life. Her friends had often marveled at how candid Warren was with her. It seemed that once their children became teenagers, they wouldn't tell their mothers much of anything. Maybe her son had just figured out that he was supposed to act this way as well.

In all, in spite of Warren taking her to a strange place with bad food, it had turned out to be a very pleasant way to spend the time. At least it was until they got ready to leave.

"Let me handle the tip," Antoinette said when Warren reached into his pocket for some money to pay the check.

"No, I've got it."

Antoinette reached for her purse. "Don't be silly. You don't need to pay for everything."

That was when she discovered that her purse wasn't there. She looked on the floor to see if she'd accidentally knocked it over, but it wasn't there, either. Her blood boiled instantly.

"She took it."

Warren removed his napkin from his lap and was sliding to get out of the booth. "Who took what?"

Antoinette nodded toward the waitress. "That woman took my purse."

"No, she didn't, Mom."

Antoinette stood, checked her seat again, and then pointed toward the waitress. "That woman stole my purse," she said loudly enough to draw the attention of people across the dining room.

The waitress was delivering a plate to another customer when she looked up to see that Antoinette was pointing directly at her. She pretended to be confused.

"You!" Antoinette said. "I know it was you!"

The woman stood stock-still, obviously horrified that Antoinette had caught her. Warren came over to take her by the arm.

"Mom, you're being a little loud."

"You don't think I should be loud about this?"

"Mom, the woman didn't take your purse."

"Then who did? It had to be her."

Warren tried to move her out of the restaurant, but Antoinette wouldn't budge.

"Mom, no one took your purse."

Antoinette turned her fury on her son. She couldn't believe he was going to let them get away with this. "MY PURSE IS GONE!"

Warren used a little more strength and pushed her toward the door. "Mom, quiet down. Everyone is looking at us."

"They shouldn't be looking at us – they should be looking for their purses. This restaurant is a den of thieves."

The hostess came toward them as Warren continued to manhandle her out of the place. "Is there a problem, sir?"

"There's no problem," Warren said apologetically.

Antoinette couldn't believe what she was hearing. "How could you be such a wimp? You're letting them steal from me!"

Warren applied more pressure to her arm and practically threw her out of the diner. In spite of her aching legs, he scurried her along and didn't let go of her until he'd forced her into the car.

When he came around to sit in the driver's seat, she glared at him. "You disappoint me," she said severely.

"Mom, the woman didn't steal your purse."

"Then who did?"

"*No one* did. You didn't have it with you."

Antoinette threw her hands up in the air. "Well, that's just ridiculous. I always have my purse with me."

Warren took a deep breath, and Antoinette could practically see his mind working as he tried to come up with a response.

"You haven't used a purse in more than a year. I don't even know if you have a purse anymore."

"Well, you should. I use the leather purse that you gave me for Christmas."

Warren shook his head slowly. "I gave you that purse ten years ago. We gave it to Goodwill when we moved you out of the house because you'd replaced it with the black one with the gold clasp."

For the first time since this incident started, Antoinette felt confused. Why would Warren tell her that he'd given her the purse so long ago? She remembered that Christmas vividly. Don had teased her about all the stuff she was moving from her old bag. The waitress was probably just going to throw that stuff in the garbage after she took her money.

Ten years ago. Why would Warren say something like that?

Her confusion fogged her anger. As Warren drove her back home, she stared out the window at the unfamiliar landscape.

She felt very tired.

NINE - Getting to Delicious

The episode at the diner had confounded Warren more than any previous event with his mother. It wasn't simply that she'd become so irrational about the purse, though that was harrowing enough. What truly upset him was the juxtaposition of her fury against the pleasantness of the conversation they'd been having earlier in the meal. This spoke volumes about where things were going.

When they'd been joking about the diner's mediocre food and reminiscing about his mother's cooking, Mom had seemed more alive than she had recently, and he'd found that extremely encouraging. When she started deconstructing his soup and analyzing its shortcomings, it was as though he was a teenager and she was in her fifties again.

Regardless of how much he'd read about his mother's disease, he continued to be mystified by the processes of the human brain. She looked at a town that she'd lived in for decades as though she'd never seen it before, but she could call up her cooking knowledge without a hitch. This had to have something to do with the way these things were imprinted on her mind, but Warren knew that the nuances of how this worked would always elude him. One thing was certain, though: his mother might have lost touch with most of the world around her, but she still felt some connection to food. Since taking her out to eat was probably too risky to venture again, Warren decided he would bring food to her in a way she never could have anticipated. He would cook for her.

Warren had grown up loving food. It was impossible to live in his home and feel differently. Something always seemed to be on the stove or in the oven, and the aromas always seemed seductive. While he attached to the family passion for dining very early, he never connected with his mother's excitement for making meals. They'd spent some enjoyable times in the kitchen when he was younger, and even when he was older he'd help her chop vegetables from time to time, but the end product was always much more appealing to him than the work involved in getting there. When he moved out, he cooked at home maybe a dozen times a year, always keeping it as simple as he possibly could. Crystal enjoyed cooking a little, so she made the meals when they weren't eating out or taking in. Since he'd been living on his own again, he'd done little more than toss some pasta with olive oil on occasion.

Now, though, that was going to change. He'd stopped at a local supermarket on the way to Treetops to buy the ingredients necessary to make one of his mother's classic dishes. He'd eaten it so often growing up that he knew the components by heart. He'd seen his mother prepare it numerous times. What made the dish so delicious was its simplicity, a point that Mom had reinforced every time someone complimented her on it. How hard could it be for him to prepare this for her?

He could do this one on a stovetop, which was important, since her apartment only had those two open-coil burners to work with. He bought the necessary groceries and drove out of the supermarket parking lot toward Treetops. That was when he remembered that his mother no longer owned any cooking tools. A quick stop at Bed, Bath & Beyond for a skillet, some tongs, and an inexpensive chef's knife addressed that.

Laden with packages, he simply smiled at Keisha as he entered, choosing not to engage in their traditional faux flirting today. He didn't even stop for a visitor's pass. The staff certainly knew who he was by now. Some of them probably even thought that he lived here, though of course he was at least twenty-five years younger than the youngest resident. He used a free knuckle to knock on the door of his mother's apartment, so caught up in his mission that he didn't anticipate the sudden dread he felt at wondering who she would be when she answered.

Fortunately, the woman that received him today was the gentle, smiling one. "Warren, honey, how are you? Do you want some tea? I was just about to make some."

Warren kissed his mother on the cheek and put the bags down on the floor near the cooktop. "Maybe later, Mom. Hey, I've decided to make us lunch. I thought I'd try my hand at making your Chicken Margaret. Sound good to you?"

"Chicken Margaret," Mom said wistfully. The expression on her face seemed a mix of confusion and melancholy. Warren had anticipated the former, but not the latter. He certainly hoped he wasn't going to wind up upsetting her with this. It was so difficult to know what her triggers were now.

"Do you think you could talk me through it?"

Mom moved to the couch and sat slowly. "I'm not sure I remember."

Warren started pulling groceries from one of the bags, placing them on the dinette table across from the cooktop. "Of course you do, Mom. You could probably make this thing blindfolded. I have chicken cutlets, rice flour, cake flour, lemons, olives, plum tomatoes." He reached for a smaller bag inside the Bed, Bath & Beyond bag. "I have vodka. You always said that Smirnoff was best for this, right?"

A tick of recognition showed in his mother's eyes. "Smirnoff is best. The expensive vodkas don't taste the same."

Warren toasted his mother with the vodka bottle, delighted that she'd engaged with this at least a little bit. Maybe he'd be able to pull her toward this gradually. He pulled out the rest of the ingredients before unpacking the skillet and utensils.

"You don't have to cook for me, honey. Don't you need to get back to work? Isn't your boss going to be upset that you're taking this much time away from the office?"

Warren stopped pulling items from the bags and closed his eyes. Did he really think that every problem was going to go away instantly because he bought some food? "Mom, I don't . . . Don't worry about my boss. We're making Chicken Margaret now, and that's all we need to think about."

Mom always named her original dishes after friends and relatives. Warren had a chicken dish of his own in his name, as well as a rice dish and two desserts. All of those seemed a bit beyond his culinary reach at this point, though. According to family legend, Chicken Margaret was one of his mother's early inventions, created not long after she'd married his father, and named in honor of her beloved sister, who'd served as her maid of honor. It was essentially an amped-up version of Chicken Piccata. Mom always served it with potato croquettes and sautéed broccoli rabe. Rice was going to have to suffice today, though. This was going to be enough of a challenge without adding complicated side dishes.

Warren washed his hands and then mixed the rice flour and cake flour together in a dish. He realized as soon as he opened one of the few cupboards in the apartment that he'd failed to consider all the necessary implements.

He found a couple of bowls and plates there, but he was going to have to use these to prep the meal and then wash them before serving the food. He opened the package of chicken.

"Season the egg rather than the flour," his mother said. She'd moved to the dinette table. Her eyes seemed brighter now than they had a few minutes ago.

Warren put down the cutlet he'd begun to remove from the package. "Egg, right." He hadn't remembered to buy any, forgetting that the chicken went from egg to flour twice before it went into the pan. He guessed he could go to the facility's kitchen to ask for a couple of eggs, though he really didn't want to draw attention to the fact that he was cooking in his mother's room. "I don't suppose I could use water, huh?"

His mother tipped her head to the side as she had when he was a kid. "No, honey. You can do without if you have to. Just dredge the chicken in the flour."

So much for replicating his mother's Chicken Margaret precisely. Warren added some salt and pepper to the flour and then dredged four cutlets, pressing them deep into the flour in hopes that this would fortify the coating in some way. Once he'd done that, he prepared the other ingredients. After he struggled to get the pit from an olive, his mother showed him how to do so with the flat side of his knife. Cutting tomatoes with a cheap chef's knife turned out to be a bigger obstacle, and Mom could offer him no solution other than to suggest he seek out a serrated knife if he were going to do something like this in the future.

With everything prepped, he set out to start cooking. He took out the rice to get that started, only to realize that he hadn't bought a pot to cook it in. Hoping against hope, he examined the cupboards again and found nothing useful. Why hadn't he and Crystal brought any of

Mom's cooking equipment here when they moved her into Treetops? They'd left her with a number of things from her kitchen for sentimental reasons – the ballerina egg timer, for instance – but they really should have thought to move a couple of pots and pans in with her simply for symbolic purposes. It wasn't an issue now. What *was* an issue was that the meal was getting simpler – and less like his mother's – by the second.

Mom called out to him as he took the chicken to the stove. "You want nice high heat for this. The cutlets are thin; they'll cook quickly."

Warren cranked the burner toward the high end and added some olive oil to the pan. Judging from how long it took to boil water in the teapot, he guessed that the stove was a low-efficiency model, but he figured he'd get some heat out of it if he waited long enough. Eventually, he added the chicken. It started to sizzle immediately, which he took as a good sign.

"You're doing great, honey."

"I haven't really done much yet, Mom."

"It smells delicious."

Warren wasn't sure about getting to delicious today. He really just wanted to do better than the diner, figuring he'd set the bar low for himself this first time. When he turned the cutlets and saw that the first side had browned well, he began to gain a bit of confidence.

All of which he lost quickly when he removed the chicken and added the vodka to the pan. The immediate vaporizing of the first drops caused him to flinch, which led to his spilling the vodka over the side of the pan.

Which led to the pan igniting.

Which led to his spilling more vodka.

Which led somehow to the handle on the teapot burning.

Which led to a surprising amount of smoke.

His mother screeched while at the same time repeating "It's okay. It's okay. It's okay" rapidly. The smoke died relatively quickly, but not before melting a sizeable portion of the teapot handle and stinking up the entire apartment.

The knock on the door came seconds later.

"Antoinette? Is everything okay in there?"

Warren, brandishing a towel to shoo away the smoke, answered the door to find Jan on the other side, looking alarmed. "We're fine."

Jan peered toward the stove. "What are you doing in here?"

Warren waved the towel in the direction of the pan, which had completely stopped sizzling. "I'm making my mother lunch."

"Here?"

"Yeah."

Jan leaned toward Warren conspiratorially. "You know, we don't really expect people to cook in their apartments."

Warren leaned toward her in the same fashion. "Then why do you put stoves in them?"

"I can't really answer that."

"You didn't call the fire department, did you?"

"I thought I'd check it out first." She smiled. "One of the attendants is coming with a really big bucket of water, though."

Warren looked back at the stove. "Is it okay if I finish this?"

Jan followed his eyes. "I think only you can answer that."

"I mean can we avoid having the authorities come down on us?"

Jan touched him lightly on the arm and smiled again. She had a great smile. "I'm not going to rat you out, if that's what you're asking."

Warren's blood pressure was slowly dropping below cardiac arrest levels. "Thanks. Want to join us?"

"That's nice of you to ask, but I just had lunch."

Warren glanced back at the pan. The chicken just looked soggy and abused now. "You would have said that if you hadn't eaten in a month, wouldn't you?"

"Not a month, no." She backed toward the door. "Have a nice meal. Maybe a salad next time."

Jan left and Warren turned back toward the stove, catching his mother's eye as he did. "I'll be ready with this in a few minutes, Mom."

"That sounds good, honey. I'm just going to put on the TV for a little while. Let me know if you need me for anything."

The rest of the dish came together without the intervention of any first responders. In the end it did-n't taste much like Warren's memory of Chicken Margaret. He'd forgotten the butter to finish the sauce as well. Mom seemed to appreciate it, but this might have simply been a case of maternal instinct kicking in.

What was undeniable, though, was that for at least a few minutes, she had seemed genuinely engaged. This adventure in cooking had been, at best, a flawed experiment. But it was an experiment worth repeating.

TEN - A Random Channel

It was past eight when Joseph and Will decided to seek out a hotel. The drive after lunch hadn't been any more illuminating than the drive that came before it. Joseph tried to make sense of the road signs, but none emerged. He took over behind the wheel about an hour out this afternoon, hoping that some sensation would tell him to take an exit or switch to another highway. All that happened instead was that Will spent considerably more time playing disc jockey. In the end, his driving was a bad idea. Since he didn't have a wallet, he didn't have a license. If for some reason a cop pulled him over, how would he explain his situation? What did they do with people who couldn't identify themselves in any way?

They chose the hotel based on a billboard they passed a few minutes after they decided to stop. The sign for the hotel sat on a busy commercial street with four lanes of traffic and endless options for shopping. The hotel itself, however, was at the end of a winding side street that left the four-story structure insulated from the sounds of cars and enterprise. Like the rest stop, this had been something of a surprise. A line of evergreens bordered the property, and benches dotted the rolling landscape, creating a parklike impression. The building itself seemed as if it had gone up yesterday, though it had a stone portico that made it feel solid and timeless.

Joseph's first thought as they got out of the car was that they'd shot too high with this place. He had a considerable amount of money in his pocket, but he had no idea how long he'd be on this journey. He couldn't waste his cash on exorbitant lodgings. What was going to happen when they ran out? It wasn't as though he could borrow from Will. As far as he could tell, the kid had never even had a paper route.

When they asked for a room, though, Joseph found the rate to be very reasonable. This proved to be even more surprising when the room turned out to have two plush beds with thick mattresses, furniture that looked an awful lot like mahogany, and marble appointments in the bathroom. Maybe they had special rates for people who looked completely lost.

"Do you have a preference for a bed?" Will said as Joseph put the toiletries they'd bought a few minutes earlier in the bathroom. They'd stopped for some clothes as well, since neither of them had anything with them.

"None at all."

Joseph walked out to find the teen taking a backward leap into the bed closest to the window. "Yep, it's as comfy as I thought it would be. I could get into living in hotels."

Joseph sat on the other bed. "I don't think most hotels are this nice, though what do I know? I have a feeling that you'd probably start pining for home eventually."

Will propped another pillow under his head. "Doubt it."

Joseph kicked off his shoes and leaned back. "All right, so we keep avoiding this conversation and now it's time to have it. What's the story with your home situation? Were your foster parents trouble?"

"Steve and Karen? No, they're great. Really, really nice people. They've always made sure I was okay. They keep the house clean, and they haven't brought in eight hundred other kids like I hear some foster parents do. Just five of us, which is pretty manageable."

"Yet as it turns out you're ready to leave town the first time some stranger comes along with a story about losing his memory and needing to find his wife."

Will shifted his head toward Joseph to reveal a sly grin. "Who says you were the first?"

Joseph threw Will and amused smirk. "My point was that things couldn't have been so great for you in that foster home if you were so eager to get out of town."

"You could give me a little credit, you know. It could be that I'm just this incredibly compassionate guy. I see you looking lost on the street and I decide to give you a hand, even if it means driving with you for hundreds of miles."

Joseph scoffed, his amusement draining away and his concern for the boy rising. "Do you always do everything you can to avoid talking about your feelings?"

Will turned to face the ceiling again. "I was ready to go, okay?"

Joseph examined the teen's face for a minute. While Will's posture suggested that he was done with this conversation, his expression said something completely different. He decided to probe further, hoping that Will would appreciate Joseph's attempts to draw him out. "What do you remember of your parents?"

For several seconds, it appeared that Will was going to stay closed on this subject. Then he slowly shifted in the bed. He was still looking upward, but he'd moved a little closer.

When he spoke, his voice was shallower than it had been before. "I remember what people have told me. I don't remember anything real. You know how you've been doing that meditation thing where you try to get a picture of your wife? I've been trying that trick since I was a kid. Best of luck with that one."

Joseph had the instinct to reach across to put a hand on Will's shoulder, but he kept it in check. "How did they die?"

"Everybody's a little vague on that one. I'm not sure how many details foster parents get. I'm not even positive that they died at the same time. It might have just been really close together. I'm sure I could dig up the details if I tried. I'm not sure it matters, though. How much of a difference is any of that going to make?"

Joseph wondered how he felt about that. If he were in Will's situation, he'd probably want every detail he could get. He'd want a vivid picture of the people who'd brought him into the world and loved and nurtured him in his earliest days. Why wouldn't Will want the same? Didn't he know what he was missing?

"You have kids?" Will said when Joseph had let the conversation rest for a few minutes.

"Was that one of your tricks to attempt to jog my memory?"

Will finally turned to face him. "Sorry, I forgot for a second. How cool would it have been if you'd said, 'Yeah, Tommy is nine and Jenny just had her sixth birthday?' I'd be a freaking genius."

Joseph let the idea rest in his mind for a moment. "No, Tommy and Jenny don't ring a bell. No one that sounds like Tommy or Jenny, either."

"Too bad. Want me to throw out names until something sounds familiar?"

"Maybe some other time."

Will sat up, reached for the television remote, and pointed it toward the TV. "Okay, here's the deal: I'm gonna turn on the TV and punch in a random channel. Whatever show comes on will give us a huge clue about where you live and where we need to go tomorrow."

Without waiting for Joseph to respond, the boy pressed some buttons on the remote. When the TV came to life, he pressed two more buttons. The scene that popped onto the screen was set on the flight deck of a spaceship. A man dressed in silver, who seemed to be in charge, was talking to a hard-shelled magenta alien.

"Is your car equipped with hyperdrive?" Joseph said to Will as the alien pounded his claw/fist on a console.

"So much for that idea. Does the name Betsy mean anything to you?"

"I'm afraid not."

"Craig?"

"There are a lot of names, you know."

"Emily? Franklin?"

Joseph held up a hand. "Let's just watch some TV. We'll pick up the search tomorrow."

They spent the rest of the night letting the television occupy them. At every commercial, though, Will would toss out a few more names. Will obviously had no intention of pursuing the conversation about his home life further, but he was going to be relentless about getting Joseph back to *his* home.

You had to admire the kid's effort.

ELEVEN - *The Other Ninety-five*

"Okay, Mom, I've cleaned up and stashed everything away so you'll be in the clear if the cooking police show up."

Antoinette had just settled into bed, pulling the sheets up around her neck. Warren came into the room and kissed her on the temple. "I'm gonna get going. Are you sure you're okay?"

"I'm fine. Just a little tired."

"I'm not poisoning you, am I? I didn't even think about that."

Antoinette huddled into the bed a little more. "Lunch was delicious, honey."

"It didn't taste much like Dave's Pasta with Shrimp, did it?"

Antoinette pulled the comforter a little tighter. "It was very tasty."

"Hey, at least I didn't set anything on fire. I'm considering that a huge accomplishment." He leaned over and kissed her again. "I'll see you tomorrow. I haven't figured out the menu yet. Did you ever make cereal for anyone?"

"Bye-bye, honey. Love you."

Warren put a hand on her back for a moment, and then left the room. When she heard the door to the apartment close, Antoinette shut her eyes and let her heart take her where it might.

. . . She was in Don's embrace, her head resting on his chest, her fingers toying with the hair on his upper arm. She could tell from the intense relaxation in her limbs and the dreamy wakefulness in her head that they'd just finished making love. As had been the case from their first night together, now eighteen months ago, Don stroked her back softly with his fingernails. This time was definitely not like every night, though. As wonderful as their lovemaking always was, this night was something beyond that.

She smoothed her hand over his chest. "Do you think we did it, Don? Do you think we started our family tonight?"

He pulled her a bit closer, though there was already no room between them. "I hope so, Hannah. I really hope so."

"Did it feel different to you?"

She felt the gentle rise of his chest as he chuckled. "You know me, darling. No matter what I'm thinking about when we start, I'm completely consumed by you within seconds."

She hadn't expected this response. "You mean you weren't thinking the entire time about our making a baby?"

He lifted his head and turned it toward her. "You mean you *were*? A guy could get a complex about that sort of thing."

She kissed his shoulder and propped herself up on one arm. "I was swooning, of course. I'm sure you noticed *that*. You never, ever, have to worry about it. But a baby, Don. A baby!"

Don smiled at her and ran his fingers through her hair. "You're not going to give this child *all* of your attention now, are you?"

"Only ninety-five percent."

He grinned at her slyly. "Do I at least get the other five?"

She pecked his cheek. "You get the other *ninety*-five. That's how this works."

"If I did the books in the office that way, I'd go to jail."

She settled back down on his chest. "This is not about offices, Don. And it's definitely not about calculations. It's about magic. Family magic. Don't you think?"

Don pulled her closer still. He was always doing this, as though the only way they could truly be near enough would be if they were in the same body. She loved it. "I do think so, darling. I think we're going to have a magical family together."

"Does three still sound like a good number to you?"

"I'm not sure," he said slowly. "Are we talking about the numbers the rest of the world uses or your magic numbers? I just want to make sure that I'm not agreeing to have eighteen children."

She pinched his side. "Just three, Mr. Smart-Aleck. Two girls and a boy."

"Unless it's two boys and a girl."

"Or that."

"Or three boys."

She let the idea percolate for a moment. "If we have three boys you're going to have to hire a nanny for me."

"As though you would let anyone else take care of your kids."

Antoinette giggled and then rose up and took Don's head in both of her hands. "Isn't this exciting?"

She kissed him quickly and he pulled her back to him for a longer, deeper kiss. "I love you, Hannah."

She kissed him again. "I love you, Don."

He held their heads close together. "You know it might not have happened tonight, right?"

"I know. And if we have to try several times before it happens, I'll be fine."

She settled in his embrace again. "But it did happen tonight."

TWELVE - Curio

Warren had hoped that the cooking aromas would draw his mother out of her room, but she stayed there instead. Over the past few weeks since he'd started making these daily lunches, her strength seemed to be flagging. He was relatively sure that there was no direct connection between the two events – in fact, only the food seemed to jostle her at all – but it was still disappointing that his attempts to draw her back into the world had so little impact. It seemed that she was walking slower than ever, and she always appeared to be tired. Warren had discussed this with the doctors at the facility, but they seemed unmoved. Their unspoken message was "She's old; what do you expect?" Warren assumed that they saw the kind of mental and physical decline she exhibited with numbing regularity; but this was a singular event in Warren's life. Dad had gone in an instant – he had driven to a Senior Citizens function the day before a heart attack felled him. He wasn't going to trivialize this, no matter how "circle of life" the Treetops staff got with him.

The dish he was preparing today was Ralphie's You-Must-Be-Kidding Pork. Mom had created it for a neighbor so obsessed with pig meat that he'd insisted his wife have their kitchen painted pink. At a casual dinner party with Ralph and his wife, Mom presented a pork loin wrapped in bacon and stuffed with kielbasa, ham, and sweet Italian sausage, served with a sauce flecked with prosciutto. The way she told the story, she'd intended it as somewhat of a joke, but everyone at the table enjoyed it so much – especially Ralph, who by some reports wept – that it made regular appearances at large gatherings.

Making this meal was definitely pushing Warren to the edges of his nascent cooking skill. He'd convinced the butcher at the supermarket to butterfly the pork for him, which was a big help. Warren did-n't want to think about how many pigs might have died in vain if he'd attempted the exercise himself. Still, the stuffing required significant preparation. The pork products needed to be chopped or removed from their cases and then mixed with minced onion, sage, rosemary, egg, and just a tiny bit of bread-crumbs. He then needed to roll and tie the pork, drape bacon over the entire thing, and roast it.

The makeshift kitchen seemed to grow daily as Warren contemplated new meals. He'd brought the one good pot he had at his apartment, along with a cutting board, a knife, and a few other utensils. When he went to Crystal's to sign their long-negotiated divorce agreement, he told her about his cooking exploits and she suggested that he take some of the pans they'd saved from Mom's house. This morning, he was already in the Treetops parking lot before he realized that he didn't have an oven in which to roast the pork. Another trip to Bed, Bath & Beyond – his fifth in three weeks – netted him a portable brick oven. It was an extravagance, especially since he was no closer to landing a new job than he had been four months ago, but it seemed in the right spirit of things.

The roast was now in the oven while Warren sautéed spinach with garlic, and boiled potatoes for mashing. His mother had taught him years ago that every entree should include a green vegetable and a starch, and now that he was feeling a bit steadier about cooking, he stuck to that with these meals, even though it meant eating a far larger lunch than he normally ate, and even though his mother only grazed through bits of it.

When he was done with the sides and while the pork rested, he contemplated the sauce. Beyond the prosciutto, he had no idea what went into it. He'd never seen his mother make this dish. Deconstructing the pork was easy, especially since the primary ingredients were the stuff of family legend, but the sauce was a complete mystery. She'd long lauded shallots, so he minced one and threw it into the pan where the prosciutto had been sizzling. Then he added some chicken broth, which certainly made the sauce liquid, but didn't come close to the right consistency or flavor. He let the sauce reduce while he considered other additions. A tablespoon of butter made it thicker, but nothing else. He was getting ready to punt. Maybe he didn't even need a sauce.

"Apple jam."

The voice startled Warren. He'd been so focused on the pan that he hadn't even realized his mother was awake.

"You finish the sauce with butter and apple jam."

Now that Warren thought about it, he could remember a slight taste of apple in the sauce cutting through the mountain of pork. If he'd really concentrated, he probably could have figured that out. Of course, he never would have guessed about the jam part. He didn't even realize you could make jam out of apples. Applesauce and apple butter, sure. Apple *jam*?

"Um, I don't have any of that."

Mom patted him on the arm with an understanding smile and moved him away from the pan. She looked in the apartment's small refrigerator and found the remains of a bottle of orange marmalade that Warren had used a few days earlier.

"It won't be the same, but it'll work," she said as she added a few spoons of the marmalade to the pan and stirred it with a whisk.

She turned to face him, satisfied. "Just let that simmer for a minute. Is everything else ready?"

He laughed, thinking about how easily she'd solved a problem that had him befuddled and thinking about how great she looked with a whisk in her hand. "Yeah, just about."

They sat to eat a few minutes later. The sauce wasn't what he'd remembered, of course, but the orange did a decent job of balancing the richness of the pork, and the pork itself had a ridiculous amount of flavor.

Though her "closer" act had been impressive, Mom ate her usual birdlike quantities. Warren had been taking the leftovers home and eating them for the next night's dinners, but even the small pork roast he'd gotten left him with a considerable amount of meat. When his mother retired to her bed about a half hour after lunch, he made up a plate and headed to the office Jan shared with the other nurses.

"I thought you might be hungry," he said as he laid the plate on her desk.

She looked up at him with an appreciative smile. "How did you know I didn't get a chance to eat lunch today?"

"I could hear your stomach rumbling all the way down the hall."

She looked down at the plate. "This looks great. What is it?"

"It's pork roast stuffed with three different kinds of pork with a prosciutto sauce on top."

"You must be kidding."

"How it got its name, actually."

She put the napkin he'd provided on her lap and then tasted the pork with the knife and fork he'd also brought for her. "You made this?"

"Well, my mother needed to come in at the last minute to save the sauce from complete failure, but I cooked the rest of it."

"Wow. I'm skipping lunch daily from now on."

"There's plenty of room at the table."

Jan tried everything and then nodded admiringly. "Did you just say that Antoinette gave you a hand with this?"

"It was another one of those moments where the decades just disappeared. She came in, fixed the sauce, and then went back to being a frail little old lady."

"That's exciting."

Warren tipped his head to one side. "It was temporary. But we've had a few of these moments. I'm thinking of putting them in a curio cabinet."

Jan reached for his hand and squeezed it, a gesture that caught him off guard completely. It took him a split second to squeeze back.

"Can you sit for a while, or do you need to get back to your mother?"

Warren pulled over a chair from another nurse's desk. They were alone in the office, the first time he'd ever seen it this quiet. "She's asleep already."

"That's good. Not the part about your mother being asleep, but the part about you having a few minutes. I hate eating by myself."

"Then come join us. Really. We have a seating at 12:45 every day. Except for the days when I make a huge mess of things."

"Yeah, maybe I'll take you up on that."

Jan ate appreciatively and Warren recounted the apple jam/orange marmalade in detail, presenting it the way someone on *SportsCenter* might. Minutes later, a crisis involving Mrs. Blake pulled Jan away and Warren headed back to the apartment to clean up.

Mom was deep asleep at this point. She didn't even budge when he kissed her good-bye. They'd had a moment, though.

THIRTEEN - Behind the Display

"Let's get off at this next exit," Joseph said as they approached a sign for a town named Vista.

Will looked over from the driver's seat, eyes wide. "You recognize something?"

"No, sorry. We've just been driving for most of the last two days. I need to get out of the car for a while. Maybe walk around a town a little. We haven't tried that yet. It could help."

The expectation on Will's face dimmed. "Sure, what the hell."

The kid took the next off-ramp and then drove left at Joseph's direction. Joseph didn't have any particular reason to make this suggestion, just as he had no particular reason why he wanted to stop in Vista, but he figured any action was better than no action at this point. Any decision, regardless of how randomly chosen, could lead to a breakthrough of some sort.

For a mile or so, this didn't seem to be a particularly fruitful choice. There had been a couple of fast-food restaurants near the exit, but the road turned residential quickly, lined with ranch-style houses on modest plots of land. Six houses in a row were painted various shades of light blue.

"We could be driving right past my home," Joseph said as they stopped at a traffic light. "My wife could be sitting right there in that kitchen right now telling someone how worried she is about me."

"You'd know."

"Would I? Why would I know? *How* would I know? The fact is, my house could have been down the block from where we started and we've just been driving farther and farther away all this time. Either that, or it could have been two exits back. What was the name of that town? Oh, yes, Greendale. Maybe I live in Greendale and my memory is just too shot to help me out in any way."

"You'd *know.*"

The strain in Will's voice when he said this surprised Joseph. Joseph had liked the kid instantly. He was easy to like, with his floppy hair and crooked smile. His commitment to the cause was definitely his most endearing quality, though. Joseph had gotten nowhere near enough of Will's story out of him, but as their time together grew, it seemed that Will's devotion to getting Joseph home increased exponentially. He was taking this personally and would no doubt consider it a huge failure if they didn't achieve their goal.

For the first time, Joseph wondered what would happen to Will if they ever did find Joseph's wife. Would Will stay for dinner and then get in his car to return to his place with Steve and Karen and his four foster siblings? Did he have other expectations or other plans? Was Will scouting out someplace for himself as they made this journey? When Joseph reached his destination, what could he do to help Will reach his?

The road began to change about a quarter mile later. A small downtown shopping district emerged, brick buildings with elongated awnings and flowering bushes on hip-high wrought iron planters.

"This what you had in mind?" Will said as he slowed the car to accommodate the heavier traffic.

"Yeah, this is just what I was looking for. Let's walk around a bit."

Will found a parking space adjacent to a shop with an orange awning. They walked toward the shop, saw that it sold dresses, and kept walking down the block.

"Do you and your wife do stuff like this?" Will said as they looked into the window of a bicycle store.

As he had with each of Will's prompts, Joseph considered this. "I don't know. Maybe. This doesn't feel strange, so I guess there's a chance."

The next store sold athletic shoes. Its window displayed dozens of sneakers, some looking aggressively high tech and others looking expensively casual.

"Oh man, they have the new Mega-Trainers," Will said, pointing. Joseph followed his finger and his eyes landed on a pair of white shoes with a thick black sole that seemed better suited to a car. There were tendrils of silver rubber reaching up toward the laces.

"You like those?"

"This is the first time I'm seeing them in person. I've been reading about them online for months. This is *the* shoe of the moment."

Joseph looked down at the boy's shoes, assuming that Will had once coveted them as much as he did the Mega-Trainers. The sneakers had some of the same markings as the new shoes, but the leather had become nearly worn through at the right pinkie toe.

"Do you want to try on a pair?"

"I don't know; they'll probably just crush my soul."

"No, come on. I need to see these up close. They'll look different on your feet than they do in a store window."

They walked into the shop and Will gave the clerk his shoe size. The clerk seemed impressed that Will wanted to try the Mega-Trainers, which probably meant that the sneakers were ludicrously overpriced. When Will tried them on, he sighed, as though he'd just stepped into a warm bath.

"Molten armor," he said.

"What's that?"

"That's how they describe these shoes. 'Molten' because they fit your feet like they were made just for them and 'armor' because you could dance on a bed of nails when you had these on without feeling a thing."

Will stood and took a series of long strides across the store, pivoting sharply and making a darting move as though he were on the field of play before walking back to his seat.

"I'd better get these off before my heart breaks," he said, reaching for the left lace.

"Leave them on," Joseph said.

Will looked at him, confused.

"Leave them on. I said I'd pay for gas. This is like gas for your feet."

"Hey, good line," the clerk said.

"Pass it along to the shoe company. Maybe they'll give us a discount."

Will stood. "You're gonna buy these for me?"

"You need 'em and they look good on you."

"Geez, really?"

Joseph put a hand on Will's shoulder, something that suddenly seemed much easier to do than it had seemed the other night. "You're driving me all over the place waiting for me to have some kind of breakthrough. I really think I can do this little thing."

"Wow, thanks."

The shoes didn't make as much of a dent in Joseph's wad of cash as he expected. The clerk threw in a sticker that meant nothing to Joseph, but seemed to please Will, which made the entire purchase seem like more of a bargain.

They continued their trek down the block, with Will making several sudden lunges forward or fast side-steps. "Yep, these shoes are incredible."

Will seemed more boyish since he put on the sneakers. It was as though the shoes that had literally given him more bounce in his step had done so figuratively as well. It was entertaining to see. Joseph wondered if something in one of the shops on this street could do the same for him.

They browsed an electronics store and bought some almond bark at a chocolate shop. At a music store, Will saw a new release from a band he liked, approached it quickly, and then turned back to Joseph, pointing and saying, "Not asking for it. Not asking."

The store after that featured a wide variety of goods made from recycled materials. They found hats made of burlap coffee sacks, drinking glasses made from wine bottles, serving bowls made from old vinyl records, and sculptures created from found objects, among dozens of other things. They'd been alone in the store when they entered, but as Joseph examined a tote bag made from old magazine covers, he heard a burst of laughter behind him. He turned to find four women joking with one another as they looked at the merchandise. He could only see the face of one of them, a brunette with wavy ringlets who appeared to be in her late twenties.

Then the woman whose back was directly toward him moved to a display on the other side of the store. She moved behind the display quickly, but not before Joseph caught sight of her. Fair, creamy skin with high cheekbones. Tiny nose, slim eyebrows, full lips, and gleaming blue eyes. Slender neck that gave her a sense of regality, and thick, lustrous, shoulder-length black hair that gave her a sense of uncommon warmth. Though the woman was no longer visible, he could see her face in a variety of poses: enraptured, compassionate, surprised, delighted, thoughtful, and sorrowful.

Compelled more than he had been since he awoke, Joseph stepped quickly toward the woman, who'd bent to examine a card at the bottom of the display. She looked up at him when he approached and her eyes met his. Her *brown* eyes. Which offset her olive complexion. The hair and the cheekbones were the same as he'd envisioned a moment earlier, but this woman looked different in most other ways.

"Hi," she said when Joseph stood five feet from her, his momentum stopped suddenly.

"I'm sorry, I thought you were someone else."

"Nope, just me."

Joseph began to back away, feeling incredibly foolish. "Sorry. Very sorry."

"No problem."

He turned to seek out Will, directing the teen toward the door. They passed the woman again and she smiled at Joseph. He tried to return the smile, but he was relatively certain it came across as more of a cringe.

"I saw her," he said when he and Will were back on the street.

"Where? In there?"

"Just now."

"Then why are we standing here? Shouldn't we be, you know, reuniting the two of you?"

Joseph shook his head quickly. "No, no; she wasn't *in* there."

Will struck his signature head-cocked, hand-in-pocket pose. "You want to start this conversation over again?"

Joseph started walking back in the direction of the car. "I got a quick glimpse of a woman in the store. For some reason, I turned her face into another face – my wife's face. It was so familiar; I can't believe I forgot it for even a second."

Will stopped and pointed back toward the store. "But it's definitely not the woman in there?"

"No, she looked nothing like her."

Will's knee bent, a half version of "the pose." "You do realize you're confusing the hell out of me, right?"

"I saw my wife while we were in the store, but my wife wasn't in the store. A woman there had some of her features, and the rest just filled in." He closed his eyes and allowed the face to take over his vision. "I can see her again. I can finally see her again."

"I don't suppose you can see her holding a piece of mail with her address on it, huh?"

Joseph opened his eyes. "No such luck. But this is good. She's with me now, more than she was before. We need to get on the road again."

"Okay, which way."

Joseph followed the planes of his wife's face, hoping for a clue. "I have no idea. I've seen her, though, Will. As beautiful as I knew she would be. She's out there. Let's go find her."

FOURTEEN - *Her Talented Assistant*

. . . The baby was playing with the peas on his high chair tray. Antoinette smiled, noting that she was fairly sure that not a single pea had made it into his mouth. Batting them around the tray and onto the floor seemed so much more interesting to the little boy. When he got older, she'd let him know that it was inappropriate to play with his food and that eating it was actually much more fun. Not now, though; he seemed to be having too much fun.

Antoinette kneaded butter and flour together to make the *beurre manié* for the chicken stew she'd been simmering. "This will help flavor and thicken the sauce," she said to the boy, who she noticed had managed to mash some of the peas on the tray. He was now examining the pulp on his right palm with extraordinary interest. "I use different thickening techniques," she said with a grin she could not have suppressed under any circumstances. "Sometimes I'll use cornstarch, sometimes arrowroot. It all depends on the recipe. This approach is the most elegant, though."

With a few rapid shakes of his hands, her baby boy had managed to fling the crushed peas back onto the tray. Now he was using his index finger to create lines with them.

"Are you telling me that you'd like to make pureed peas with me? I was planning to sauté them with onions, but a puree could be nice, also." She knelt down next to the high chair so their heads were at the same level.

"What do you think? Should we mash them with some cream and cinnamon?"

The baby cackled and ran his fingers through the green mass he'd created. He then reached his hand toward Antoinette's mouth. She let him feed her some of the pea mash, which he seemed to enjoy doing.

"Umm, delicious!" She pretended to consider the taste carefully. "We might want to add a little more salt, don't you think?"

He waved his arms wildly again, which Antoinette interpreted as "And maybe a little white pepper."

"Very good point! Proper seasoning is an art and you already understand it. I knew that my baby was a genius."

She stood up to finish the meal. Both sides of the family – eighteen people in all – were coming over today to celebrate her sister Rachel's birthday. That meant multiple entrees, four different side dishes, an elaborate salad, and the chocolate cake with raspberry filling her sister had specially requested. Antoinette had been cooking since seven this morning. She knew she would be exhausted tonight and hoped that Don would offer up one of his luxurious foot massages, but right now she was working with the energy that she always felt whenever she was preparing a big dinner party. Her son had been with her for most of the work, sometimes in his high chair, sometimes crawling around on the floor, often in her arms. Throughout it all, she'd described everything she was doing to him, looking forward to the day when he would become her talented assistant in the kitchen.

Having a baby had turned out to be so much harder than she and Don expected. She'd even begun to believe that it would never happen, though her heart broke every time she allowed herself to think that. Now that her beautiful little boy was here, though, she knew that the wait had delivered its reward. When she'd held her son for the first time, she didn't think she had ever seen anything so perfect, and she still felt that way – even if at the moment her perfect child had green mush in his hair. She'd let him get as messy as he wanted right now; they would be taking a bath together in a few minutes anyway.

An hour and a half later, everyone was seated around the elongated dinner table. Don raised his glass, and everyone joined him, except the baby who was too busy trying to stuff a slice of bread up his nose. Yes, she had work to do with this one about the proper appreciation of food. It was going to be difficult to give him this lesson, however, if she giggled through the entire thing, and, above everything else, the boy knew how to make her giggle.

"I'd like to wish my sister-in-law the happiest of birthdays. Somehow all the women in this family look younger every year. I'm not asking how it happens, but I did want you to know that I noticed." Everyone laughed and Rachel thanked Don and told him that he'd just earned an extra night of babysitting from her. Glass still raised, Don turned toward Antoinette. "And to my remarkable wife, I want to offer a toast to the wonderful food she's made for us today. Hannah, you never cease to amaze me."

Cheers went up around the room, but then ended quickly, as people set out to fill their plates. Antoinette knew there would be little conversation for the next fifteen minutes or so, other than the occasional comment on the meal. They would linger at the table for at least an hour afterward, catching one another up on the events of the week or the news outside their doors, but while they ate, they said little. Antoinette took that as the ultimate compliment . . .

"I'm afraid you're going to have to accept that the lucid moments are going to become briefer and less common."

"I'm not sure how much briefer they can be. I can barely get a good fifteen minutes with her now."

"This is never easy. I've been doing this a long time and I've never come up with anything to say to make family members handle this any easier."

Antoinette opened her eyes to find her son standing next to her bed with one of the doctors. She could tell that Warren was worried about something. Ever since he was a baby boy, he'd worn the same expression – a look of total confusion – whenever he was upset.

"Hey, Mom," her son said when he saw her looking at him. "Dr. Cantor was just checking on you."

Antoinette's eyes moved to the doctor, who reached out to take her hand.

"How are you feeling, Antoinette?"

"I'm lovely," Antoinette said, thinking back on the birthday feast she'd just enjoyed with her family.

The doctor squeezed her hand softly. "I'm very glad to hear that."

"Do you want to sit up, Mom. I was trying my hand at Rachel's Cornish Hen with Spring Vegetables."

It was nice of Warren to cook for her, but Antoinette was still full from the meal. "I don't think so, honey. I'm going to close my eyes again, if that's okay with you."

"It's okay, Mom. You rest."

FIFTEEN - *Closely Intertwined with the Taste*

Warren placed the electric skillet on the dinette table and turned it on medium high to preheat. The electric pressure cooker was there as well, along with the electric rice cooker. Warren hoped he didn't blow a fuse with all of these electrical appliances. The Treetops staff had been extremely understanding about his cooking in his mother's apartment the past six weeks. Several people even asked him what he was making whenever he walked in with groceries. They'd probably be less understanding, however, if he knocked out the power down the entire hall. Still, he could only accomplish so much on two burners, so he'd expanded the kitchen the only way he saw possible. That he was spending money on all of this equipment while he still wasn't sure what he was going to do for income once his severance ran out was something he preferred not to consider. At least while he was doing this, he felt as though he had a purpose. It was getting tougher to feel this way about the hours he put in networking, distributing his resumé, and cold-calling.

Today's dish was an exercise in orchestration that he'd been hesitant to make until he got his skills up: Paul's Potent Beef. Mom had named it after Warren's best childhood friend. Growing up, Paul hung around for dinner at least a couple of times a week to avoid the enervating combination of his mother's pallid cooking and his father's cutting dismissiveness. Though Mom liked having just about anyone in their extended circle around for dinner, she was especially fond of Paul because of his over-the-top effusiveness about her meals. That Paul was deliberately doing this to guarantee that Mom kept stuffing him mattered little to her, and she'd paid him the ultimate compliment when she gave this dish its name.

Paul loved big flavors and Mom loaded them on here in a manner that rivaled her most extravagant offerings: beef braised in rice wine, soy sauce, and hoisin sauce, served on a bed of ginger and scallion rice, and topped with a sauté of blackened corn, red bell peppers, cherry peppers, and dramatic levels of garlic. She would then top *that* with frizzled shallots. She first made Potent Beef the day after Paul's thirteenth birthday. That night, Paul spoke with Warren in all seriousness about the possibility of Warren's parents adopting him. This wasn't the first time they'd had this conversation, but it was by far the most insistent time. The dish became Paul's day-after-birthday meal every year after that through Paul's final year in college. Mom even made it a second time that year to celebrate Paul's graduation a week after Warren's.

What she didn't realize at the time was that this would be the last meal she ever made for the kid who'd spent so much time at her dining table. Paul left for Southern California only a few days after college ended. As it turned out, a location across the country wasn't nearly far enough away from his parents. He moved south of the border and married and divorced a Mexican woman within nine months. After that, he was in Costa Rica until he turned twenty-six, his letters becoming far less frequent and his details of debauchery becoming far more alarming. A year later, Warren heard that Paul had wound up in a Colombian jail on a drug charge. Though Warren tried to learn more, he never heard from or about Paul again. It still mystified Warren how the relationship with the best friend he'd ever had ended with such a whimper.

For years after Paul disappeared from Warren's life, the idea of eating Paul's Potent Beef seemed wrong. While it was a great dish, and while Warren had himself requested it a couple of times on trips home from college, he couldn't do it once Paul was gone. Feelings about losing his best friend were too closely intertwined with the taste of the dish. As the years went on, though, the memory mellowed, and Paul's Potent Beef became a reminder of basketball games played, girls lusted over, cars raced on the highway, and lengthy philosophical conversations about things teenaged boys found deadly serious. Mom seemed glad to put the dish back into the family rotation, and it showed up several times at the twice-monthly Sunday meals Warren shared with his parents.

As was the case with so many of the lunches he made in his mother's apartment, Warren hadn't eaten Paul's Potent Beef in years, since his mother had stopped cooking. Still, his memory of it was especially strong. To cook it today, he made a few modifications to Mom's recipe. She'd always used chuck roast; he was using boneless short ribs instead. He replaced the cherry peppers with fresh Anaheim chilies because they looked good to him in the store. She'd always simmered the meat in a low oven for hours; he was using the pressure cooker because long simmering meant sitting – in all likelihood alone, given his mother's current condition – in her apartment all that time. Otherwise, he would try to make it the same way she always had. His imitations of her work had been getting better. The tastes he was able to coax from the kitchen seemed increasingly similar to the tastes his memory generated.

The electric skillet was hot now, so he added a considerable amount of canola oil and, a half-minute later, the thinly sliced shallots. While they fried, he tossed the vegetables on the cooktop, tasted, and added a bit more ground coriander. He actually could have cooked the shallots on the cooktop as well, as he had an available burner, but things never got particularly hot there. Warren guessed this was by design, as it minimized accidents among the elderly – though, as he knew from experience, it couldn't prevent all of them. Regardless of how much progress he'd made as a cook, the memory of his first smoky mess persisted.

Warren took the shallots out a minute later, draining them on some paper towel. He looked at the mass of machinery and cutlery around him. Cleanup was going to be a bear this time.

All to make a meal for himself.

It had been nearly two weeks since his mother last ate anything Warren cooked. In the brief periods when she was both awake and lucid while he'd been with her, she'd been willing to eat very little, usually some crackers and a bit of fruit juice. He'd continued to hope that the smells in the room would pull her back – it had happened before; it could happen again – but he'd been able to generate no such magic recently. She'd taken a sharp decline both physically and mentally and Warren was beginning to lose any sense of optimism for her revival.

He put a mound of rice on a plate and added two short ribs from the pressure cooker, which he'd cooled and depressurized. On top of this, he spooned vegetables. Warren remembered asking his mother if it wouldn't have made for a neater presentation to put the vegetables on top of the rice and the meat on top of that. Mom acknowledged that it would but that such a presentation wouldn't be anywhere near as exciting. Back then, this hadn't made terribly much sense to him, but as he plated the food himself, the logic kicked in – she wanted the dish to seem as though it were toppling from sheer over-load. Finally, he scattered shallots over the plate by hand.

The food looked and smelled great. This had been by far his most complex project to date and he was pleased that – at least by appearances – it had turned out so well. A forkful later, his taste buds corroborated.

He walked with the plate to the entrance of his mother's bedroom, waving the scent in her direction with his hand. It was a stupid attempt at "sorcery" and it had the predictable results. Mom's body remained inert.

Warren sat to eat, feeling that his culinary accomplishments today had been especially hollow. No one made meals like this to eat alone. He took another bite, wondering if it made sense to continue to pretend that cooking this way had some function. He put down his fork, suddenly wondering if even *eating* the food he cooked had some function. Caught between the quality of his accomplishment and the emptiness of eating alone under these circumstances, he stood up, grabbed his mother's keys, and walked down to Jan's office.

The nurse who was definitely the Treetops staffer he'd gotten to know best had obviously just returned to her desk with her lunch. She was reaching into a drawer to pull out a spoon when he arrived.

"Step away from the yogurt and no one gets hurt."

Jan looked up at him, spoon aloft.

"That's not really lunch," he said. "I have a significantly better alternative for you."

Jan held up the yogurt container. "You have something better to offer than Yoplait Banana Cream Pie? How is this possible?"

Warren gestured with his hands to suggest that the container go back on the desk. "Trust me. Will you join me for lunch?"

Jan got up from her chair and began to walk with him down the hall. "I have to tell you that I've been jealously smelling whatever you've been making for the past hour – some of the residents are starting to get envious, by the way – and when I went to get lunch *nothing* seemed good to me. That's why I got the yogurt. I was trying to convince myself that I was getting a treat."

"Hey, I've been there. Did you know you can make popcorn seem like dinner if you sprinkle enough parmesan cheese on it?"

Warren opened his mother's apartment door for Jan and directed her toward the couch as soon as he realized that the dinette table was too much of a mess to allow two people to eat. He put together a second plate from the various cooking implements and put both of them on the coffee table.

"This looks amazing," Jan said when he sat across from her. She shifted her eyes toward his mother's bedroom and her expression softened. "She's just sleeping through it again?"

Warren nodded slowly. "She always does now. I don't think I had her for more than five minutes today."

Jan looked back in his direction. "I spoke to her doctor yesterday."

"I'm sure what you talked about wasn't any more encouraging than the conversation I had with him two days ago."

"I'm afraid not. Sometimes people rally." Jan pursed her lips before she continued. "It's not common, though, Warren. I'm not going to try to kid you about that."

Warren appreciated the honesty, though he really would have appreciated Jan's honestly being able to offer him a sunnier scenario. "I know. I'm working incredibly slowly toward accepting that."

"Have you thought about a nursing home?"

Warren cringed. "Have you ever seen a nursing home?"

Jan dropped her eyes. "I know."

Warren let the thought linger for a few seconds. Then he moved forward in his chair and reached for his plate. "I didn't ask you here to bring you down. I can mope on my own. This is about lunch." He pointed toward her food. "Why don't you give it a try?"

Jan offered him an expression that he interpreted as compassion over the difficult exchange they'd just endured and then picked up her plate and tried the beef. Her eyes grew wide. "This is incredible." She let the taste linger. "And there's a whole lot going on here."

"Mom was shooting for layers of flavor when she concocted this. That, after an immediate punch in the mouth."

"I definitely felt the punch – and the layers. Is that Anaheim chili?"

"Wow, yeah. Are you a chili head?"

Jan flipped her bangs. "I'm more of an everything-edible head."

Warren surreptitiously examined Jan's slim form and wondered how someone who professed to love food that much could be in such sensational shape. "And yet you were going to have yogurt for lunch."

"I don't think you heard me. It was *banana cream pie* yogurt."

"Does that really matter?"

Jan took another forkful of meat, digging into the plate to get some corn, some pepper, and some rice at the same time. "I didn't know this was an available option," she said before putting the overloaded bite in her mouth and pretending to swoon.

"This is always an available option."

"Don't make promises you can't keep," Jan said around her food. Very few people looked good talking while they were eating. Jan happened to be one of those people.

"I'm serious."

Jan met his eyes. Warren's immediate response was discomfort. He'd meant the comment to be a casual one, but it didn't sound that way coming out of his mouth.

"I really am serious," Warren said, deciding to plow ahead. "Look, I think the only thing sadder than me taking two hours to cook lunch and then eat alone is you having yogurt at your desk. I think we have the potential for a win-win situation here."

Jan seemed to think about this for a while. It dawned on Warren that his offer might have come across as more presumptive than he intended it. Were there even rules that prevented this sort of "fraternization" between staff and the children of residents?

Before he could say anything more, though, Jan said, "Okay" quickly, and then returned to her lunch. She ate several bites hungrily and very fast before she spoke again. Warren found he enjoyed watching her eat, especially since she was exhibiting so much passion for something he'd created.

"You know, we could split my yogurt for dessert afterward."

"That's very generous of you."

She took two more rapid forkfuls and then seemed to realize that she was eating very fast. Her shoulders relaxed and she put the plate on her lap. "Have you been making meals like this every day?"

"I think I hit my stride in the last week. You wouldn't have wanted to try what I was cooking before then. Culinary Russian roulette."

"Sounds like it might have been exciting," she said with a teasing smile. "So what's on the menu tomorrow?"

"I don't know. I don't usually decide until the night before. Do you want me to e-mail you with my decision?"

Jan took another bite and then moved the plate from her lap to the coffee table. "Definitely not. I like surprises. And this has been a very pleasant surprise."

"For me, too," Warren said, marveling at the dramatic way his spirits had shifted in the past few minutes.

SIXTEEN - The Other Side of the Glass

The road seemed particularly endless today. Charged by the vision he'd had of his wife's face, Joseph had had no trouble staying enthusiastic for a long drive yesterday. However, when he woke this morning and accepted that he hadn't gotten any closer physically to the woman he loved, the weight that had been building on his shoulders as his travels continued returned. There was no possible way for him to mark progress. Therefore, the vision he now had in his head, which he was convinced was the woman he was seeking, was nothing more than an especially beautiful mirage. He even had to acknowledge that this vision could be a matter of his mind playing tricks on him. Maybe the picture he now had in his head wasn't accurate in any way. Maybe he'd just invented the woman's face because he desperately needed to visualize something.

When they got into the car, Joseph let Will choose the direction they headed. The simple reality was that his instincts hadn't helped much. Maybe the boy's doing the equivalent of flipping a coin would be more useful. Realistically, he couldn't do any worse than Joseph felt he was doing. Will chose a two-lane road that cut through a collection of small towns. This led them through minor business districts followed by little clusters of houses followed by vast expanses of farmland. At least the view was more varied than it was on the big highways they'd traveled. Under different circumstances, he might even consider this a pleasant little drive.

As usual, Will took charge of the music selection. He'd offered Joseph the opportunity on several occasions and asked for his opinions on a number of others, but Joseph was fine with the arrangement. It was Will's music, it was Will's car, and he was doing the driving. Whatever he wanted to listen to would be fine. Right now, Will was playing a rock band named The Raconteurs. Joseph didn't find the sound very appealing, but Will seemed to love it, elaborately miming guitar playing on the steering wheel. He wished he could be entertained that easily.

Joseph tuned the music out – in Joseph's mind, the kid's tastes were wildly inconsistent – and watched the landscape out his side window. Soon, this seemed to disappear for him as well, becoming a blur, though Will was driving relatively slowly.

"I miss you so much. I can't do this without you anymore."

The words – from a female voice – seemed to be coming from just on the other side of the glass. His senses alive again, Joseph looked to the front and the back of the car, as though doing so would offer some kind of clue. He even looked over at Will, who was in the middle of a guitar solo and seemed to have his eyes closed while he was doing it.

"I think about you every minute. Where are you?"

Was this another trick of the mind? Was Joseph's desire to be with his wife so extreme that his imagination was getting the best of him and he was now hearing voices in his head? How much longer would it be before he started hallucinating nonstop?

"I'm right here," he said tentatively, not sure if he actually spoke the words aloud.

"Really? Is that really you?" The voice went up a register in excitement. "You sound so real."

"I am real. I'm right here in this car. I'm lost and I'm trying to find you."

"Come home soon. I need you with me all the time."

Joseph felt tears coming to his eyes. It was her. It was most definitely her. This was not a mirage. This was not a trick of his mind. It was her voice, she was distressed, and he wanted more than anything to ease her mind.

"I'm trying, but I don't know where you are. We're driving all over the place. I had some kind of accident and my memory is gone. How can I find you?"

"I'm home."

"But I don't know where that is."

There was a long pause and Joseph wondered if he'd lost the connection. He searched the landscape, hoping to see her somewhere out there. He hadn't been this close to her since he woke up in that strange house. He wanted to hold on to this link with everything he had.

When she returned, her voice was thinner.

"I don't know how to explain it to you."

"Give me an address. The name of the town. We'll figure out how to get there."

Joseph waited for a response, but none came. Maybe they were going through the equivalent of a bad reception area. Maybe she would come back soon. When several minutes passed, Joseph wondered if the problem was that the car was in motion. If she came back, he'd ask Will to stop driving until he finished his conversation.

"I'm still here," he said, certain now that he was speaking aloud.

He waited again.

"I'm still here," he said more forcefully, this time banging on the window as if that would help broadcast the message.

He felt a hand on his shoulder. "Are you okay?"

Joseph turned sharply toward Will. "No, I'm not okay."

"You've been talking to yourself for the past few minutes. What's going on?"

Joseph felt the intensity drain from him, replaced by weariness. "I wasn't talking to myself. I was talking to *her*."

Will turned down the music. "You were talking to your wife?"

Joseph looked out the window, then back at Will. "You think I'm insane, don't you? It was her. I know it."

"I'll take your word for it. Did she tell you where she was?"

"She's home."

"We kinda knew that already. Did she happen to mention where home is?"

"She said she didn't know how to explain it to me."

Will watched the road for several seconds and then tilted his head back in Joseph's direction. "Did you at least get her name?"

Joseph felt himself drain further. "No, I didn't."

"Damn."

"Yeah."

Joseph rested his head on the side window.

"You're connecting with her, though. First that thing with her face yesterday and now this thing with her voice. That's gotta mean something, right?"

Joseph didn't answer. Instead, he hoped against hope that he'd hear her voice again.

SEVENTEEN - *Tired*

Antoinette awoke with a start, her vision blurred, her senses rattled. She was so frustrated to find herself back in this bed that she wanted to scream.

Suddenly Warren was at the door. "Mom? Mom, are you all right?"

Antoinette didn't know how to explain it to him. She didn't know what to say. Everything was always so confusing these days. Nothing stayed in one place for long.

He was at her bedside now. Taking hold of her hand. Helping her to sit up. Why did he think she wanted to sit up?

"Are you in pain? I've never heard you scream like that before."

Pain? She didn't notice the pain she felt the same way anymore. It was always there, but somehow she couldn't really touch that, either. Everything was vague. Her entire existence was vague.

"Are you hungry?"

Antoinette looked at her son, unsure how to say what she wanted to say, how to tell him what she really wanted. "A little thirsty," she said thinly.

Warren left and came back a minute later with some juice. She took a few sips, which felt better than she thought it would.

But why couldn't she stick with anything? Why did everything float in and out? If she knew where she wanted to be, why couldn't she stay there?

Her son held a plate in front of her. "I made Ellie's Chicken Pie today. I think it turned out okay. Do you want to try some?"

Her eyes went to the fork in his hand, but she made no effort to move. The idea of eating confused her now.

"Let me give you a taste. I did a couple of things differently from the way you did it, but it's basically the same thing. Ellie probably would have liked it."

He scooped some food with the fork and brought it to her mouth. Antoinette opened slowly and allowed herself to taste the food. Like the juice, she enjoyed this more than she expected. She remembered Ellen, the babysitter who came on Saturday nights when Warren was little. He always called her "Ellie."

She swallowed. She felt a little more awake now, a little less agitated. She still wanted to go back to sleep, but she wasn't as frustrated with being up as she had been.

Warren gave her another bite of the chicken pie. Did he say he made this? When did Warren start cooking?

"Is it good?"

Antoinette nodded and sipped some more juice. When Warren brought another fork full of food to her lips, though, she turned her head away.

"Do you want to get up for a while?" he said, putting the plate on her nightstand. "I think *Password Plus* is on in a few minutes."

"I'm tired."

"You've been sleeping all day, Mom. It might be a good idea for you to get around a little."

Antoinette slipped back down into the sheets, closing her eyes. She hoped Don would be there to welcome her.

EIGHTEEN - Running in the Red

"I've gained three pounds since we started doing this," Jan said as Warren put the plate in front of her. Today's dish was Sole Vanessa, named after his mother's niece who was more than twenty years older than Warren. He'd simmered the fish slowly in clam broth, preserved lemon, and pink peppercorns, and then topped it with a puree of piquillo peppers and parsley. On the side, he had Brussels sprouts roasted with bacon and almond wild rice.

"It must be three pounds of muscle," he said, sitting down across from her.

"I wish. I think you're bad for my health. This looks delicious, though." Jan took a taste of the fish and sighed appreciatively. "Yum. This is a different flavor profile for you."

"It is. Not that I ever used the term 'flavor profile' until recently. Did I tell you I've started watching the Food Network at night? Do you know anything about chayote? Someone was doing something with it on one of those competition shows last night and I thought it looked interesting. Anyway, I realized that I'd been tending toward my mother's more muscular dishes, probably because those tended to be my favorites. I thought I'd go for something a little subtler this time, extend my range a bit."

Jan took another bite and then tasted the Brussels sprouts. "Delicious."

She raised her water glass toward Mom's room. "Antoinette, another winner!"

"She always loved this one. I think she liked it even more than Vanessa did. You know, it dawned on me the other day that I haven't eaten some of these dishes in more than a decade. What I didn't think about until today is that it has to have been several years since *she* ate any of them. Once she stopped cooking, no one made them for her." He sipped water and looked down at his plate. "And now she won't ever eat them again." He felt the wave of emotion that always came to him when he talked to Jan. He really didn't want to get maudlin right now, but he didn't seem capable to avoiding it.

Jan put down her fork and reached across the coffee table to squeeze his hand. Though she'd touched him before, it was the first time she'd ever done anything like that. Surprisingly, it made him sadder.

"She didn't recognize me when she woke up this morning," he said. "I let myself in, as I have been doing for a while, and I started prepping lunch. When I heard her shifting around in bed, I went to say hello. She seemed very nervous about having a guy in the apartment with her."

Jan tipped her head toward him. "She may have just been disoriented."

"No, it was worse than that. I tried talking to her and she remained very uneasy. Then she just went back to sleep. Is such a sharp decline common?"

Jan took a few moments before answering. When she'd done this in the past, he was never sure whether she was trying to think of an answer or trying to find the best way to spare his feelings. "It's not unusual. Especially when there are physical problems and mental problems at the same time."

Warren turned toward the bedroom door. He'd found himself staring at it regularly the past week, as it was the only form of communication with his mother available to him. "This has just been the worst freaking year," he said, still looking in that direction.

"You seem to be going through an awful lot at once."

Warren turned back toward Jan. Her eyes captured his instantly, as though she'd been standing beneath him with a safety net. He found unusual comfort there. It had been a long time since someone had been able to soothe him with a glance.

"Yeah, you could say that. Crystal, the job, my mom. It's not like I couldn't handle any one of those or that any of them were a surprise. Crystal and I hadn't been working for a while, the company had been running in the red for the past few years, and Mom started showing signs of her age seconds after Dad died. It's the confluence that makes this so tough."

"You're a whole lot stronger than me. I think I'd be hiding under my bed if it were me."

"Something tells me that's very far from the truth."

Jan's eyes glittered. "Let's just say I can appreciate how difficult this must be for you."

"Thanks." What she said helped. Simply being in this moment with her made a difference. "Did I tell you I got a job nibble yesterday?"

Jan sat forward. "No, that's great news."

"At least it's *some* news. To say that the market is a little cool right now would be greatly understating it. I spend a few hours every afternoon working contacts, and this is the first even marginal sign of interest I've gotten."

"I can't believe I don't know this, but what do you do for a living?"

Warren considered the question for a second, since he wasn't currently doing *anything* for a living. "I was a vice president at a holding company."

"Sounds serious."

Warren scoffed. "I was a middle manager for a corporation that owned other companies. Essentially I supervised supervisors."

"And there aren't a lot of jobs for supervising supervisors right now?"

"There aren't a lot of jobs for anything right now."

"Oh, I definitely know that. I say a little thank you every time I walk into my office and see that my desk is still there." She chuckled to herself and then said, "Do you like this 'supervising supervisors' thing?"

Warren had only asked himself that question a few thousand times in recent years. "I think I'm fairly good at it and, you know, people tend to like things that they're good at, I guess. My father was great at it. He considered managing an art form. I think I let his enthusiasm rub off on me."

For as long as he remembered, Warren had admired his father. He took his life seriously and yet still seemed to enjoy every part of it. The guy talked about his job as though he were running the State Department, seemed to know everything that was going on in Warren's school and social lives, and treated Mom like she were the heroine in some forties musical. That was one heck of a parlor trick and Warren hadn't fully appreciated how difficult it was to accomplish until he'd become an adult himself.

He realized he'd stopped talking in mid-thought. When he looked at Jan, it became obvious to him that she was waiting for him to finish.

"I don't feel I've actually *done* anything. Managing is just so vague. I mean, you *do* something every day."

Jan responded with an exaggerated nod. "I do, I do. Yesterday, I helped Mrs. Patel find her teeth. Today, I helped Mr. Larson change out of wet underwear. I hear they're going to give a Nobel Prize for that next year."

Warren held up a hand. "Nope. I can disparage being a middle manager, but you're not allowed to disparage being someone who helps people. We have to have some ground rules here. I looked this up online the other day. Do you know that nursing is America's most trusted profession?"

"I did know that. We tend to remind ourselves of that as we try to pay the bills." She paused and appraised him. "I'm a little surprised that you know it, though."

Warren tried to treat this casually. "A person can only do so much networking in a day."

She let it pass. "Is this nibble for a new job similar to your last job?"

"Broadly speaking. *Very* broadly speaking. It's a division manager position for an auto parts company."

"That could be fun. Are you a car guy?"

"I *have* a car."

"Sounds like the perfect fit, then."

There was a bit of rice left on Jan's plate and she scooped up the last of it. A couple of days ago, she let a couple of broccoli florets go unfinished and Warren considered this to be a statement on his skills with the vegetable.

"If you get this job, I guess you won't be fattening me up anymore," she said.

"First of all, *Janice*, you are decidedly not fattening. I think another of our ground rules needs to be that you don't ever have to worry about the way you look. I mean, really. And second, the office is only a couple of miles away. I'll bring you takeout."

Jan got a look in her eyes that Warren couldn't read clearly. "It's January."

"What?"

"Jan isn't short for Janice. My full name is January."

This struck him as surprisingly revealing. Warren guessed that nearly everyone Jan knew assumed that her full name was Janice. "Do you have eleven siblings?"

"Only two. And, no, my little sister's name isn't March."

"January. That's nice. Why don't you use it?"

Jan shrugged. "I shortened it in school to fit in. It just stuck."

"I guess we all do that sort of thing."

Jan's mind seemed to drift a bit, but then she focused back on him. "So you'd really bring me takeout?"

For the second time today, Warren felt embraced by Jan's eyes. Rather than feeling comforted this time, though, he felt a level of uneasiness that he did-n't particularly mind. "If you wanted me to."

"It wouldn't be the same as your cooking."

"Actually, I hear the place down the block makes a mean Sole Vanessa."

"I'm sure they do." Jan looked at her hands for a second. For the first time since they'd been having lunch together, Warren wasn't sure where the conversation was going to go next. He found this disorienting in all the right ways.

Then Jan stood quickly, reaching for the plates. "Hey, we'd better clean up so I can get back to my desk. You never know whose teeth I'll need to find this afternoon."

NINETEEN - *Strangely Recognizable*

Another day, another hundred miles in the morning. Joseph had stopped wondering if he was going in the right direction or even whether he should direct Will or let Will go wherever he wanted. Though he'd had more than his share of frustration, his experiences the last couple of days suggested that what he needed to do more than anything else was just let these experiences come to him. He couldn't actively seek clues; he just needed to be available when they showed up. He had fewer expectations about a revelation in a road sign. Instead, he waited for another message; something similar to the vision in the store or the "conversation" with his wife.

Will still seemed determined to get him where he needed to go, wherever that was. He'd tried talking to the boy about his latest observations, but Will seemed to be more comfortable with the idea that they were headed *someplace*. Will drove with his usual sense of purpose. After some time on the highway, he exited and started winding down a smaller road.

"Shouldn't someone your age be thinking about college right around now?" Joseph said as Will played music from a band named, aptly enough, The Alternate Routes.

"Yeah, that's what I've heard."

"You're not buying it?"

Before answering, Will took a moment to pluck out a few notes on his steering wheel guitar, bending the last note dramatically. "It's hard for me to think of myself as a college student."

"Because you don't like school?"

"School's fine. I'm just not sure what *more* school is gonna give me. I don't think that where I'm supposed to go next has anything to do with professors."

Joseph tried to get a fix on this notion. As happened during every conversation he had with Will, he tried to draw back on his personal experience. But while the day-to-day of life seemed natural to him, his memories of what he'd been through and with whom he'd interacted continued to be nothing more than an itch in the back of his brain. His immediate reaction was that Will's attitude about his future did-n't feel right, that he was selling himself short in some way, but he couldn't tell if he was reacting this way because of what he felt he knew about the boy or because of some inner sense based on experience.

"So where are you supposed to go?"

Unlike before, there was no hesitation this time when Will answered. "I think I'm supposed to make something."

"Really? You mean like a carpenter?"

"Not that, I don't think, though I'm really good with power tools. I can absolutely kick butt with a band saw. That's not what I was talking about, though. I think I'm supposed to create. This probably sounds ridiculously vague to you, but I still haven't figured some things out. Did I mention that I play guitar?"

Joseph watched Will's fingers dancing on the "fretboard" of the steering wheel even as he spoke. "I might have guessed that."

"So I'm thinking that what I'm supposed to do could be a music thing. Or it could be something physical. I made this, I don't know, *structure* out of sheet metal a couple of months ago and it just *sang* to me. You know?"

"That would be great."

"Yeah, it would. Or I could go some other way completely. I don't have it all down yet, obviously. But I have this really strong sense that I'm supposed to make something that people can use in some way, whether it's songs or structures or dishwashers or whatever."

Joseph found Will's sense of animation exciting. The kid was a fascinating combination of nonchalant and driven. Things obviously mattered to him, but he didn't care about things casually. He was either fully engaged in something or not engaged in it at all.

For the first time since he'd found himself in this situation, Joseph wondered about his own job. Was his employer wondering where he was? Did they call home to talk to his wife when he didn't show up for work the day after he showed up in this other place instead? Did his wife update them after Joseph "talked" with her yesterday – and if so, how did she explain that conversation?

Strangely, it didn't feel as though he were missing work at all. There was no little tickle in his brain about a job. Was he unemployed? That didn't seem right, either. He was really looking forward to his memory returning so he could stop asking himself so many questions. Meeting new people could be very enjoyable, but the enjoyment paled quickly when the new person was yourself.

A few minutes later, the road narrowed and they turned toward a large open park filled with kids throwing balls and flying kites. Joseph hadn't even noticed the weather when they left this morning, but he now saw that the day was bright and cloudless.

"You hungry?" Will said.

"I'm getting there."

Will pointed off to his left. "The second I saw that hot dog truck, I got very hungry. I think that truck has something I need."

"Hot dogs in the park sound good to me."

Will parked the car on the opposite side of the street from the truck and they walked over. Joseph ordered two hot dogs with grilled onions, spicy mustard, and sauerkraut, while Will took his with ketchup only. Joseph found the idea of a hot dog with ketchup extremely dull, but he kept his opinion to himself. Goading the kid to eat more adventurously had been a fruitless exercise so far. Obviously, this was not something in which Will engaged.

They took their food to a bench near the park's playground. As they sat, a large dog with tight black curls galloped up to them and sniffed at their food. Will started to tear off a piece of his bun for the dog, but just then a slim young woman in very skimpy running shorts came up to retrieve the animal, throwing a leash around him.

"I'm so sorry," she said. "He's an escape artist. Especially if there's any food around. He's figured out how to slip off the leash."

"Quite all right," Joseph said as the woman scolded the dog and pulled him away. Joseph noticed Will watching the woman's legs as she headed deeper into the park. He couldn't blame him; the woman had lovely legs. He tried to think of his wife's legs, but nothing came to him, though he knew instinctively that the woman he loved looked at least as good as this woman when she wore skimpy shorts.

"Do you have a girlfriend at home?"

Will broke his stare, though he seemed to do so reluctantly. "I'm keeping it casual at this point."

"That was a beauty."

Will looked off in the distance again. "Yeah."

"The dog, I mean. A standard poodle, I think."

Will looked over at Joseph coyly, the wry grin in full bloom. "Yeah. Standard poodle."

Joseph chuckled and took another bite of his hot dog.

It truly was a gorgeous day out, the warmest of their trip. Joseph felt less inclined to stay in motion than he had previously. It was as though his body were telling him that it needed some time on this bench, just listening and watching. Was this a good thing, as he tried to suggest to himself earlier, or was it a sign that he was resigning himself in some way?

He glanced over at the playground. Two kids were attempting to climb a rope ladder at the same time, each trying to reach the next rung first. At a curving slide, one little girl was preparing to go down while a little boy tried to get up it from the bottom at the same time. They tumbled off together, stood looking a little dazed, and then ran off to the next piece of equipment.

Just to the left of the playground, a father was offering encouragement to a toddler sitting on the grass. "Come on, Liam, you can do it. Come walk to Daddy."

The boy pounded the ground excitedly with both hands, waved them wildly in the air, and started crawling toward his kneeling father. The man stood, offered a finger to his son's outstretched hand, and helped the boy get to his feet. Then he let go gently, backing up several paces. The boy teetered for a second, but stayed on his feet. The man reached out his hands and offered more encouragement, but for maybe ten seconds, the toddler didn't budge.

Then he took a tentative step forward, his face taut in concentration. With his second step, his knees started to buckle and it appeared that he was going down. However, the boy managed to straighten up, taking three more steps into his father's arms. He giggled as the man swept him up and twirled him.

Joseph found the vision transfixing, only noticing that he'd been holding the last of his second hot dog a few inches from his mouth after the father took his son to a baby swing to push him. The scene he'd just watched seemed so familiar to him. Had he done something like this with his own son? Did he even have a son?

"We should probably get going," Will said, putting a hand on his shoulder.

"Yeah."

Joseph ate the last of his food while still watching the man and the toddler. He could hear the tinkle of the boy's laughter every time his father pushed him a little higher.

Will patted his shoulder again. "You wanna go?" Joseph reluctantly stopped watching the man and baby and stood. He turned to gesture toward Will to let him know that he was ready.

But the Will he saw now was not the Will who had been his impromptu traveling companion for the past four days.

The Will he saw now was both strangely recognizable and achingly foreign.

TWENTY - *Squeezing Her So Tight*

. . . Antoinette had asked Don to come with her to this meeting with the doctor. She was horribly worried that the news would be bad, and she didn't know how she'd be able to handle it alone. For nearly forty years, her body had worked in such predictable ways, but in the past couple of months that had changed. Two years ago, Ralph's wife Theresa had died of cancer, and Theresa's symptoms had started in a similar way. Antoinette had no idea what she'd do if she had to face the same disease. Theresa had been in so much pain at the end. And what would Don do? He was strong in so many ways, but could he stay strong if he knew she was that sick? What would it do to him to watch her life fade away? She couldn't allow herself to think this way; she had to keep a positive outlook. What the doctor had to say to her now didn't have to be awful.

Dr. Turner was a tall, stately-looking man with huge hands. His graying, receding hairline gave him the appearance of an academic, but his soft, warm eyes always made him seem very approachable to Antoinette. She knew that if he had something dreadful to tell her that he would do so as gently as he possibly could.

"Your palms are sweating," Don said as he squeezed her hand while they waited in the doctor's office.

Antoinette leaned toward him, touching her head to the side of his. "Sorry."

Don kissed her hair. "It's going to be okay, Hannah. Whatever he says to us today, it's going to be okay. We're going to be all right."

The door opened behind them and Antoinette and Don got up from their seats. Dr. Turner shook their hands and then sat behind his desk. His eyes and his relaxed expression helped soothe Antoinette's anxiety the tiniest bit, though she knew he was a professional and would always look this way to his patients.

"You're not sick, Antoinette."

Antoinette melted in her chair at those words. It felt like someone had just covered her with a warm blanket.

"You're pregnant."

What Dr. Turner said so stunned Antoinette that she was sure she heard him wrong. If that were the case, though, Don wouldn't be squeezing her so tight right now that she couldn't breathe.

"Oh, my god, Hannah," he was saying. "Oh, my god. I'd completely stopped hoping. I'd just come to accept . . ."

The rest of what he was trying to say remained unspoken. He hugged her even tighter and then kissed her full and long on the lips. Antoinette could still barely believe what was happening. After all the heart-break, she'd never even considered this possibility.

"I'm pregnant?" she said to the doctor.

Dr. Turner smiled broadly now, his eyes shining brightly and sending off even more warmth. "You're definitely pregnant, Antoinette. I hope that makes you happy. It certainly seems to have made your husband happy."

Antoinette looked at Don, seeing an expression on his face that she'd never witnessed before. He'd always looked at her lovingly. There was softness in his eyes even when they argued. But what she saw now nearly caused her heart to burst with emotion. Don was looking at her as though she were some kind of miracle. As though heaven itself had just smiled down upon them.

"Don, we're going to have a baby."

Then she was in his arms again and the full force of the doctor's news hit her. There would be a baby in their home again. Seventeen years after tuberculosis had stolen their little boy when he was only fourteen months old, they would once more have a child. For so long, they couldn't even think about trying again, and then when they did, Antoinette could-n't conceive.

But now . . .

She started sobbing and Don held her to his chest.

"After all these years," she said.

"I know, darling. We'd stopped hoping. This is such a blessing."

She looked up at Don, reaching to hold his face in her hands. She hadn't realized until that point that Don was crying as well. "I've missed him so much. I'll never stop missing him."

"That will never go away. How could it possibly go away? How could we ever want that? But this – this – is a remarkable thing."

A laugh burst forth from deep inside of her, shaking her with its power. She'd certainly run the gamut of emotions in the past few minutes, hadn't she? "It *is* a remarkable thing, Don. Remarkable."

Dr. Turner cleared his throat and rose from his chair. "We have some things to discuss. Pregnancy at your age is a little more complicated than it was when you were younger. But we can get to that another time. For now, I'll just leave you alone to savor this moment. Congratulations."

With that, he left, patting her on the shoulder as he did.

"I think we just kicked the doctor out of his own office," Don said.

Antoinette laughed again. There was so much to think about. They had family and friends to tell, a room to clean out for the nursery, and a million little things to do before the baby arrived.

For now, though, the only thing she wanted to do – or even *could* do – was let Don hold her. As excited as she was about everything, she needed to be here right now. She needed to feel this because she had been so convinced that she would never feel it.

TWENTY-ONE - *More Feelers*

Warren had given long thought to whether he should try making Warren's Apologize to the Neighbors Chicken before he did it. The cooking aromas were very strong. Very, very strong. The first time Mom made it, Warren told her that he could smell it while he was playing outside at a friend's house, which was how the dish got its name. Mom was being facetious then – the neighbors didn't seek apologies, though they regularly sought invitations to dinner – but he wondered if he might not be apologizing to the people at Treetops for days after making this in his mother's apartment.

In the end, he decided to forge ahead. He'd made many meals for Jan at this point, but he'd never made her any of the dishes Mom had created in his name. And he was decidedly cooking for Jan now. Warren no longer had any illusions about serving this food to his mother. She hadn't had a bite of anything he'd made since the tiny bit of Ellie's Chicken Pie he'd gotten into her when she woke suddenly a few weeks back. If that were truly the last home-cooked food his mother ever ate, he wished it could have been something more sumptuous and something with more personal resonance. If he had only known, he would have made one of her favorites. Maybe he even would have taken the ultimate risk and tried to create a dish in her name. That would have been the proper tribute, the kind of dedication appropriate to someone who'd dedicated so much to others. It was not to be, though, so his only alternative was to continue cooking in her name.

He browned chicken pieces in the fat rendered from a half-pound of bacon. He did this in the electric skillet, knowing he could never get the sear he wanted on the apartment's stove. Warren had only recently started to cook the occasional dinner at home – he was usually too full from lunch to need anything other than a salad or some soup – and he was delighted to learn that his own stove was considerably more potent. Only a couple of months ago, having a powerful stove at home wouldn't have mattered to him at all. When the chicken was brown, he removed it from the skillet and added the peeled cloves from two full heads of garlic, allowing them to get a bit of color and to, as his mother used to say, "stink up the place." Then he returned the chicken and bacon to the pan, added a bit of chicken broth, and allowed the entire thing to simmer for an hour. The intense smells of the garlic and bacon filled the room; it was aromatherapy for gourmands.

Normally, he would have tried to speed things along with the pressure cooker, but he had something else to do with the time today. The job prospect that had seemed so promising had ended with an insulting offer – slightly more than half of what he'd been making before – so he'd brought his laptop with him to send out more feelers while the flavors in the chicken developed. He'd do more of this when he got back to his place later, but he wanted to get a jump on it here.

When the hour passed, Warren added some chopped tomatoes and let them cook into the sauce for forty-five minutes. By the time this happened, he'd sent his résumé to a dozen new HR departments and had joined his fourth social networking site for corporate professionals. When Jan arrived, he threw pasta into a pot of boiling water and stirred a few tablespoons of heavy cream into the chicken.

"I've been smelling this all morning," Jan said, "and now I'm ravenous."

"The question is whether the people on the highway or maybe in the next town have also been smelling it all morning."

"A definite possibility. Mrs. London asked me today why the food coming from the kitchen always smelled so good and then tasted so plain. I didn't have the heart to explain it to her. Have you thought about putting a catering truck outside? I'll bet we could negotiate it into the residents' meal plans."

"Thanks for the idea. I'll work on that."

Jan walked into Mom's room, emerging about fifteen seconds later. "I just wanted to check on her. She seems comfortable, though her breathing is still a little shallow."

Warren had never seen Jan with any of the other residents, so he had no idea if she was like this with everyone, but the caring look on her face after she tended to his mother always touched him. She took her job incredibly seriously and she was sure the people in her charge felt it, even if many of them had minds as clouded as Mom's had become.

"If I stay in there with her for a while, I notice that it cycles. Sometimes her breathing quickens and sometimes she's very still."

Jan looked back into the room, seeming contemplative. That could mean so many things, some of which were welcome and most of which were not. She turned and offered him a narrow smile that required no interpretation. After a moment, though, she brightened.

"So, what's on the menu."

Warren told her the name of the dish.

"She made this one for you?"

"She did."

It suddenly seemed to Warren as thought they were crossing some kind of threshold with his presentation of this meal. Since he always told Jan what he knew about why a dish had its name, she understood what Mom tried to capture when she created something original. Therefore, presenting Jan with Warren's Apologize to the Neighbors Chicken was a form of inviting Jan to see him as his mother saw him. He hadn't considered that when he'd decided to make it today, and now he found himself reviewing every step he'd taken. He certainly hoped he'd cooked the dish properly. There was no time to worry about that now, though. Jan was here and lunch was ready.

Warren put Jan's plate in front of her and her eyes widened. "Wow, it's even more powerful when you serve it than it was in the pan." She grinned at him. "Were you particularly . . . fragrant when you were a child?"

"I'll never admit to that."

She cut a piece of chicken and tasted, reacting with the level of appreciation he'd come to anticipate from her but never fully expect. "Oh, I get it, you were an especially *delicious* child growing up."

Warren's face warmed and he hid it by getting up to retrieve a jar of crushed red pepper. "Give it some of this," he said, handing her the jar. "It completes the assault on your senses."

Jan shook on a few flakes and tasted again, nodding to acknowledge that his recommendation had been a good one. "How close is this to what you remember?"

Warren took another forkful of chicken and then tasted it again with the pasta, allowing himself to go back to his first memory of the dish when he was in elementary school. It had been an entirely ordinary spring day, warm enough to play outside after school. When his mother served it for dinner that night, the flavors hit him immediately. It took longer than that, though, for the import of his mother's naming the dish for him to sink in. That day, she'd said that she wanted to make something very dramatic in his name because that would show him how dramatic his place in her heart was. At the time, he'd passed this off as the kind of soppy thing mothers said to their kids. He wasn't thinking that now.

"I think it's pretty close."

"That says a lot."

"Is this going to be another stinky joke?"

Jan smiled and sat back in her seat, her eyes sweeping him up, as they so often did. "I was going to say that I could taste your mother's love for you in it."

The comment affected Warren especially strongly. Since he'd begun replicating the food Mom served, he'd thought about the fun she had creating these culinary monuments to family and friends. Now, though, he flashed back on the look of excitement in her eyes when presented his plate and told him the name, or the pleasure that she reflected when he would subsequently request the dish. She desperately wanted him to love this food, because if he did, he was accepting much more than nourishment from her.

Surprisingly, he felt his eyes get misty. He lowered his head and attempted to blink this away.

Jan reached across the table and took his hand. She didn't squeeze it or pat it. Instead, she just held it. "You must have been such a gift to her, her only child coming at that stage in her life."

Warren looked up at Jan and then down again at their entwined hands. She was reaching across the table, which had to be uncomfortable for her. While he didn't want to let go, he squeezed her hand once and then released it. Jan smiled softly and then picked up her fork.

"I wasn't her only child," Warren said.

Jan's fork paused in midair. "You weren't?"

"I had a brother. He died a long, long time before I was born. He was only a little more than a year old."

Jan looked over Warren's shoulder toward his mother's room. "That must have been terrible for your parents. Was it some kind of accident?"

"Tuberculosis. I heard the story from my mother and father so many times that I feel like I was there. There was less than a week from the time they found out he was sick to the time he died."

Jan put a hand to her mouth and shook her head slowly.

"I showed up seventeen years later."

"Wow. You really were a gift."

"I'm not sure they felt that way when I entered puberty."

"Try that line on someone who hasn't known your mother for a few years. My guess is that she *always* saw you as a gift."

Warren ate some more pasta, savoring it with newly tuned taste buds. "I hope so. My brother was a pretty cute kid."

"Was he?"

"Yeah. They had pictures of him all over the house. Everything from my mother bringing him home from the hospital to him taking his first steps only days before he got sick. He was adorable, though I probably wouldn't have thought so if he were beating me up all the time." Warren pointed toward a sideboard under the window that held a number of framed photographs. "That's him over there all the way to the right."

Jan went over the sideboard and bent to get a closer look at the photo. Then she looked at the photo next to it.

"Is this your baby picture?"

"Yes, it is."

"You were cute, too."

"Please. I was a late bloomer. At that age, I looked like my Uncle Sal. Some people were convinced that I could fly by flapping my ears."

Jan giggled. "You're going to have to bring in more pictures tomorrow."

"We could pull out my mother's photo books. I'm amazed she never forced you to sit down with them. She did it all the time when she was still in her house – the neighbors, relatives, the UPS guy."

Jan returned to the couch quickly, her face blooming with excitement. "Let's do it now."

Warren held up a hand. "No, I'm afraid that's not going to happen," he said with mock sternness. "We're going to need a little *quid pro quo* here."

"What are you talking about?"

"If you want to see more of my childhood pictures, I'm afraid you're going to have to bring in some of your own."

"No, no, no. That's not a good idea."

"Come on! Don't tell me you're self-conscious about them. You were probably this supernaturally beautiful child that caused people to run into walls when they saw you."

Jan's eyes grew big and she blushed. Thinking about what he'd just said to her made Warren blush as well. Unfortunately, getting up for more red pepper wasn't an option, so he was just going to have to play this out.

"Okay," she said with an exaggerated tone of concession. "I'll bring in a couple tomorrow. A couple of *very carefully selected* pictures."

"Then we have a deal."

Jan had to get back to work a few minutes later. Before she left, she kissed him on the cheek and thanked him for the lunch. She'd been doing that for a while, but something felt different when their faces touched this time. Her skin felt warmer; he suddenly realized how intimate it felt to have her this close. And as he started to clean up, he couldn't help but notice the sense of lightness that accompanied his movements.

As he started to remove the leftover chicken from the skillet, an idea stopped him. Rather than putting the chicken away, he added some water to the pan and turned the power back on. The intense aroma of the food had been comforting and maybe even a little incantatory today. He wasn't ready to let go of it yet. He had his computer with him and he didn't need to be anywhere this afternoon. He could do everything he needed to do from here. He'd let the chicken simmer a while longer, casting its distinctive scent throughout the apartment.

When he finished cleaning everything else, he visited his mother's room. As had been the case the last time he checked on her, she seemed deeply indented in the bed.

He kissed the cool skin of her forehead. "Hey, Mom. I have some of my chicken cooking." The smell of the food had gotten stronger even in the minute he'd been there. "I love that you were thinking of me the first time you made it. Let me know if you want some."

TWENTY-TWO - *Bordering on Overpowering*

Joseph kept glancing over at Will as they drove. Since they'd left the playground, he'd been contemplating a scenario so disconnected from his instincts that he couldn't even think of addressing it aloud. So little of it made sense, and like the majority of his thoughts since he'd awakened without his memory, all of it was hazy. He was still chasing after moments of clarity. Something would sharpen for an instant, but then very quickly become lost in murkiness.

One notion had continued to grow stronger since they'd watched the toddler in the park taking his first steps: Will was not simply the helpful stranger Joseph had been assuming he was the past five days. They had a very different relationship, one that Joseph couldn't fully identify and of which even Will might be completely unaware. While Joseph was now convinced of this much, the murkiness made it impossible for him to see it any better than that.

Joseph didn't realize he'd been staring at the boy until Will turned to him and said, "What's up with you? It's like you're trying to burn a hole into my head with your eyes."

Joseph looked away, setting his sights on the road instead. They'd come to a large commercial district, stopping at traffic lights every thousand or so feet. "I was

just admiring your handsome profile," he said, attempting to be casually jovial. "Is that a problem?"

"Well, yeah, actually it is. That's also *not* what you were doing. You're thinking about something. What is it?"

"I was thinking you should change the music. This stuff is awful. Put on that Ari Hest guy again."

Will didn't touch the music, which meant he was-n't buying this at all. The teen focused on his driving, and for the next ten minutes, neither of them spoke. Then, still not saying a word, Will turned into a strip mall and parked the car.

"I'm getting hungry," he said, pulling his keys from the ignition. He removed his seat belt and Joseph did the same, moving to open his door. Before he could get out, though, Will shifted toward him and spoke again.

"Look, Joseph, we're partners in this thing. I'm not driving you all over the place because I didn't feel like finishing a science project in school. I know something's going on in your head. I've seen you do this before. You kinda owe it to me to tell me what it is."

Joseph had marveled at the teen's commitment to this quest before, but this was the first time he'd heard Will say anything about their being "partners." This jogged his mind a little further – but still not enough to discuss the wild notions that were going through his head.

"You're right," he said. "I am thinking about something and I owe you an explanation. But this isn't like the woman in the store or the conversation I had with my wife. I think it's bigger than that, but it's also much more vague. I can't talk to you about it until I figure out a way to put it into words."

Will seemed satisfied with the explanation, though it sounded like empty evasion to Joseph's ears. The teen studied Joseph for a few seconds and then turned toward his door and got out of the car.

Will had pulled up to the equivalent of a diner, even though it wasn't a freestanding building. The interior looked like a luncheonette from the early fifties, complete with Formica countertops and waitresses in crisp black uniforms. Joseph had been to places like this before, though of course he couldn't remember a single one. It looked like the perfect restaurant for Will to get the simple food he seemed to prefer. Joseph had tried to challenge the kid to eat something with more flavor, but he'd been entirely unsuccessful. By this point, Joseph figured he'd just let Will eat whatever he wanted. Will was a big boy and he certainly didn't need Joseph standing over him telling him to eat his vegetables or try something exotic.

As expected, Will did a quick scan of the menu when they sat down and then turned his attention to the tableside jukebox.

"Let me guess: mac and cheese?"

"Burger and fries," Will said, intent on the song choices available. "You have a couple of quarters I can use?"

Joseph reached into his pocket and gave Will the coins, then perused the menu looking for anything that suggested a personal touch from the chef. Even places as simple as this sometimes had a specialty of some sort. As he searched, a powerful cooking smell seemed to rise out of the menu. Joseph looked up from his reading, now noticing that the smell seemed to fill the entire restaurant. It was intense, bordering on overpowering, but it also awakened his appetite in a surprising way. There was garlic – quite a bit of it, it seemed – and something smoky. And some kind of meat; maybe pork, maybe chicken.

Joseph hadn't been particularly hungry when he got out of the car. Now, though, he definitely wanted to order whatever was filling his nostrils. The only problem was that the item didn't seem to be on the menu anywhere. There was no shortage of choices – sandwiches, meat loaf, roast turkey, Salisbury steak, and many others – but absolutely nothing that suggested the intensity of that aroma. Nothing sounded anywhere near that good.

"What do you think that is?" Joseph said to Will, who'd made his music choice and was tapping out his accompaniment on the jukebox.

"What do I think *what* is?" the boy said absently. He obviously had one more choice left for his money and he flipped through the available selections.

"That smell."

Will raised his nose to the air and then shrugged. "Diner smell?"

"Have you ever smelled anything like this in a diner before?"

Will smirked. "Only in every diner I've ever been in."

Frustrated, Joseph turned back to the menu. When the waitress came, he asked her to tell him what was cooking in the back. She looked at him blankly, and Joseph attempted to describe the aroma to her as clearly as he could. Like Will, she didn't seem to smell it. He asked her to go in the kitchen to find out if the cook was doing anything special, maybe trying out something a little different, and she laughed, saying, "Mister, we haven't had something 'a little different' in here in fifty years."

Joseph wasn't satisfied with this answer and the waitress's casualness miffed him. The scent had awakened something in him that went beyond hunger or simple interest in a new taste. He didn't just want to try this food; he wanted to *experience* this food. If the waitress wasn't going to help him – and it was obvious that she didn't intend to do so – he'd help himself. He stood up and headed toward the kitchen. This caused the waitress to call out after him. Ignoring her, he went through the double doors that separated the kitchen from the dining room.

On the other side, three men in white shirts stared at him simultaneously. One was frying burgers on a grill. Another was chopping up vegetables for a salad. The third had been pulling plates from a dishwasher. None seemed to be associated in any way with the smell that had driven Joseph here. He took another step toward the flattop, hoping to spy something that he couldn't see from the entrance to the room.

A woman came around the corner. Like the others, she was dressed in white. Though she was dressed the same, she carried herself in a way that made it obvious that she was in charge. "Can I do something for you?"

He walked over to confront the woman. "You're cooking something."

She put a hand on her hip and gazed at him blankly. "That's very perceptive of you."

Joseph ignored the sarcasm. "You're cooking something that isn't on the menu. I'd like to order that, but I don't know what it is."

The woman looked at him as though he were talking another language, then turned to the other men. Then she faced Joseph again.

"I have no idea what you're talking about."

Joseph stopped for a moment. The scent was still very strong in the air. It was impossible to miss. "You don't smell that?"

The woman switched quickly from baffled to resolute. "Look, mister, we don't let customers into the kitchen. We could get in trouble."

Suddenly, Joseph was angry. He was convinced they were hiding something from him, though he had no idea why a restaurant would ever hide food from a customer. The woman had come from around the corner. Maybe there was another cooking station there. He brushed past her and then veered off to the left.

All he saw was a door. Thinking that, for some reason, there might be another kitchen behind this one, he opened the door – which led outside to a dumpster and a small parking lot. He took a few steps out, trying to make sense of this. When he looked back at the door, the woman was there.

"Mister, you'd better not come back in here. Like I said, we don't let customers into the kitchen. And I don't take kindly to people bumping shoulders with me when they walk past."

With that, she pulled the door closed, leaving Joseph in the dimming twilight.

He stepped beyond the dumpster and onto the lot. The lot was fenced off, and on the other side of the fence was another shopping center. The cooking smell intensified as he moved closer to the fence. Maybe there was a restaurant over there as well. If so, they should apologize to their neighbors on this side for filling the air with something so much more appealing than anything the restaurant over here was serving.

Joseph stopped at the fence in an attempt to get a better look. He put his hand on the top of a post.

But the hand he put there wasn't *his* hand. It was wrinkled, bony, and age-spotted. Like his father's when he was an old man.

Joseph stared at the hand, and as he did, he began to bow forward, as though gravity were suddenly exerting stronger pull. His muscles slackened and his knees bent of their own will. His breath felt short, though that might have been because of the crazy things that were happening to him. With his left hand, he touched his cheek, feeling lines he knew weren't there this morning.

He staggered to the curb and sat, covering his face with his sinewy hands. Through it all, the smell was still there. Chicken, not pork. Bacon. Tomatoes. And more garlic than it seemed possible to put in one dish.

My son was always asking my wife to make this for him.

Joseph opened his eyes and stood. He looked at his hands again, finding them smooth. His knees felt strong. His posture was straight. He took a deep breath, reveling in his ability to draw in so much air, and filling his soul with a smell that was both indescribably delicious and terribly bittersweet.

Then he made his way back around to the front of the shopping center, reentering the diner from its customer entrance.

Will looked at him with a start. "You went through that door," he said, pointing, "and you came back this way. Did you suddenly feel like going for a walk?"

Joseph studied the boy, seeing him fully now for who he was. He wanted to hug him, but he was sure it would make Will uncomfortable and maybe even cause a reaction he definitely didn't want.

Instead, he dug into his pocket, put some bills on the table, and said, "Come on. I know where we're going now."

TWENTY-THREE - *Something in Swahili*

Eventually, Warren got around to cleaning up from lunch. He'd left the chicken cooking on very low heat for three hours, during which he'd reached out to a number of new job resources and watched an *Iron Chef America* battle on the Food Network. He'd added water to the sauce a couple of times, but it still seemed overdone and unappealing when he finally unplugged the electric skillet. These would not make good leftovers. Instead of putting them in a container, he would have been better off throwing them out, but he stored them anyway.

Unsurprisingly, his mother didn't move in her bed the entire time.

It was nearly five o'clock. Traffic was going to be awful on the drive home because he was leaving Treetops so late. The twenty-minute trip back to his apartment could easily turn into forty-five at rush hour, and rush hour was unavoidable at this point. Warren wondered if Jan was still around. He knew she got to the facility early, which suggested that she also left early. He could easily imagine her becoming involved with one of the residents and losing track of time, though, which meant she could certainly still be on the premises.

He wasn't sure how he would get by right now in his life without their daily lunches. The weekends seemed endlessly long here when she wasn't around. At this point, spending time with her ranked as one of his few reasons to look forward to any day. His mother was slowly disappearing in front of him, his work prospects were fading in the same way, and Crystal continued to spar with him, even though their divorce was now official and negotiations were therefore meaningless. If not for Jan and the lunches he shared with her, he would be utterly directionless right now.

A couple of nights ago, he'd gone out for a drink with Steve Wilkins, a friend from his old office who'd been downsized at the same time as Warren. Like Warren, Steve had not found another permanent position, but he'd managed to put together a series of consulting assignments that were bringing in more money than the company had been paying him. After Steve spent the first half hour of their conversation trying to persuade Warren to consider consulting – something that made little sense to Warren under his circumstances – the conversation moved on to the rest of their lives. This quickly led to Warren's telling Steve about his cooking exploits and his lunches with Jan.

"Hey, it's good to see that you're back in the game, my man. How long have the two of you been dating?"

"Oh, we're not dating."

Steve looked at Warren as though he'd just said something in Swahili. "You have lunch with this woman every day."

"Well, not weekends, but yes."

"And you talk with her about stuff that actually matters to you."

"More and more often, yeah."

"Is she okay looking?"

"I could look at her all day."

Steve laughed uproariously. "But you're not dating her."

It seemed ludicrous when Steve put it in that context, but Steve was ignoring some key factors. One was that Jan was a nurse responsible for Warren's elderly and very sick mother. For all Warren knew, Treetops might strictly forbid their dating. Another was that Warren didn't feel anywhere near ready to get involved with another woman. The slow fade he'd experienced with Crystal had left romance an increasingly distant sensation. It wasn't so much that he'd lost interest in having a new relationship as that he'd tamped down the feeling. He'd once heard that people who experienced chronic pain slowly shut off the nerve endings responsible. Any healing that came after that usually involved a sharp spike in agony first, as the nerve endings came back online. Did he really want to have any part of that?

At the same time, it was ludicrous for him to think of Jan as a casual lunch date. People didn't have lunch together five times a week *casually*. They'd both approached this in a nonchalant manner, but at this point, Warren was building his day around it. A few weeks earlier, a crisis regarding one of the other residents had slammed Jan and forced her to skip their lunch that afternoon. Warren had felt completely thrown by the experience, unable to enjoy anything the rest of the day. He'd even had trouble eating, which usually only happened when he had a fever over a hundred and two degrees.

He wondered what Jan thought of all of this. He knew she hadn't been seriously involved with anyone since she'd split with her live-in boyfriend a little more than a year ago. They'd been together four years, and when she spoke about him, her sentences slowed and her eyes drifted downward. Had she sworn off men because of this? Were their lunches together an ideal social exercise, allowing her the flirtation and storytelling that came at the beginning of a relationship without the burdens of the relationship itself? If he suggested that they go to a movie together some night, would she run from the room?

It was so hard to know.

It didn't help, of course, to have grown up in a household with his parents. They were always touching, teasing, and engaging each other. The parents of most of Warren's friends seemed to have relationships that ranged from business arrangements to indifference to open hostility. Not his. The married couple in his home had actually seemed to like each other. They'd seemed to revel in the time they had. This had become even clearer to Warren when he'd went off to college. The first time he returned from school, his parents fussed all over him, but they also catalogued their exploits during the time he was gone. They were like kids who'd been left with the run of the house.

Warren knew that living with this had provided him with a very solid foundation. But it had also set the bar for romance very high. He never dated as much as his friends, and for a long time, he couldn't understand why. Ultimately, though, it dawned on him that he'd subconsciously decided that a relationship was only worth pursuing if he believed it had the potential to match his parents'. For a while, he'd thought he had that with Crystal, but it turned out not to be the case at all. How did you ever really know?

Maybe it was time to stop thinking this way. Lowering his standards could make his future considerably easier than his past had been. But then he thought of Jan again and realized he didn't *want* to stop thinking this way. What he wanted was to believe.

Warren was about to scoop the rest of the chicken into a food storage container to bring home (where he would likely throw it out, eventually) when he heard movement from his mother's room. The sheets rustled and the bedsprings creaked. Putting down the container, he went to her door to find Mom sitting up in bed, her legs over the covers, staring directly at him.

"Hey, Mom," he said, finding himself surprisingly anxious at the sight of his mother in an upright position.

The expression on her face languidly morphed into one of surprise, as though she were operating in slow motion. This compounded Warren's feeling that this was all somewhat surreal. Was he having some sort of hallucination brought on by his desire to see his mother awake again?

Her face shifted again, this time to a smile that formed as slowly as before. The smile wiped years from her face and Warren found tears coming to his eyes. Earlier, he'd wished for one more meal with her. Now he realized he'd be satisfied with this smile. He wouldn't be greedy enough to wish for anything more.

"You're here," she said, her voice honeylike, the voice he remembered from his schoolboy days when she would greet him as he came in from the bus with an enveloping hug followed by a glass of milk and one of the baked goods she was always making.

No longer stuck in place, he went to her bedside. "Yes, I'm here, Mom. Can I get you anything?"

But her eyes didn't follow him. Instead, they stayed fixed on the doorway, still bright and still accented by her smile.

"You're here," she said again.

That's when Warren realized that she wasn't seeing him.

TWENTY-FOUR - *Right Here*

"You're here."

Antoinette knew she wasn't dreaming this. She could feel it in her body. She reached her hand outward. The effort required to do so, and the shakiness as she held it aloft, confirmed this for her. She felt so horribly weak. This didn't matter now, though.

Don was here.

He walked to the side of the bed as quickly as his arthritic knees would carry him, the strength in his eyes as powerful and embracing as she remembered it.

"I'm here, Hannah."

He bent slowly toward her hand, kissing it gently, and then returning it to her side, so she didn't need to try to hold it up any longer. Thankfully, he didn't let go.

He looked across the bed compassionately. Antoinette followed his eyes and saw that Warren was staring at her, speechless. He obviously couldn't see his father, which was a shame for both of them. A reunion, no matter how brief, would have been good for both of them. She wanted to say something to ease Warren's mind, but she couldn't seem to get the words out. She hoped he understood.

She turned back to Don. He was looking at her now, telling her everything she needed to know through his eyes. That had always been the case. Even as the years had withered his physical strength and lined his face, his eyes had retained their brilliance and their ability to communicate in a language that spoke to her intimately and with complete clarity.

"This has been a very long five years," she said.

Joseph seemed stunned. "Five *years*? I've only been gone five days." He looked around the room, his brows lowering. "But you're here. And Warren has gray at his temples now."

He dropped his head, displaying the thick, silver hair she remembered running her fingers through on the last day they had together before today. "Five years."

"I'm glad you made it back."

Don's eyes softened further. "Me too, Hannah. You don't know how much. I think I'm only visiting, though."

Antoinette tried to squeeze his hand, but she did-n't have the strength. "I know, my love. I wish it weren't so, but I'm sure it's true."

She looked away from him, glancing down at the foot of the bed where her old housecoat lay. "I don't belong here anymore, either."

Don leaned across and kissed her forehead. She smelled the summer they'd spent on Candlewood Lake when Warren was a baby. "Maybe it's time for both of us to go home."

"I would love that, Don. I would so dearly love that."

He kissed her again, and then sat next to her on the bed, pulling her hand into his lap with both of his. "Hannah, I've had a traveling companion. I did-n't begin to realize who he was until yesterday. He's seventeen now and he's done a lot of growing up on his own, but he's a very good kid. You'd be proud of what he's become."

Antoinette felt the first tear roll down her cheek. "Billy?"

"Our Billy. He's been driving me all over the place. He's a very good driver. He gets that from his dad. We had quite the moment when we both realized who we were. I don't know which of us was more shocked.

I've been getting to know him these past few days even though I didn't know who he was until a little while ago. I think that's one of the things I needed to do before I could come to find you."

The tears continued to come, but Antoinette neither tried to stop them nor tried to wipe them away. "I want to see him."

"And he desperately wants to see you. He could-n't come in, though. It seems he can't do what I've just done for reasons I can't begin to understand. That's what worries me about all of this – I don't know if I'll be able to come to you again."

Antoinette held their clasped hands to her damp cheek. "Don't go without me."

Don nuzzled closer to her. "I'm not going anywhere, Hannah. I'll stay right here with you. As long as I can, I'll stay right here. I know what being without you is like now and I never want to go through that again."

Once more, Antoinette was starting to feel heavier. For a few moments, her body wasn't weighing her down. But it couldn't last. Now she found that she could barely keep her head up. "I'm very tired."

"I know, my love. Go ahead and lay down. I'm not letting go of you."

* * *

Warren watched his mother with a mixture of fascination and aching sadness. She was talking to "Don," the name she always used when talking to his father. His being Don and her being Hannah was all part of their mythology, one more thing he admired about their romance and that he'd always wanted to experience for himself with a woman he loved.

As she talked, his mother's voice was thin, her movements labored. It seemed remarkable that she could even conduct a conversation, given how frail she seemed and how much effort every word required. She hadn't said this much in his presence in more than a month. Of course, the fact that she was saying it to his father, a man who'd been dead for more than five years, cast a melancholy glow over every syllable. When Mom started crying as she mentioned Billy's name, Warren felt tears come to his eyes as well. Was this an act of wish fulfillment from an addled mind, or had she somehow reached out to Dad and the brother Warren had never known? Was this dearest of her dreams in the process of coming true? Though he couldn't know for sure, he would allow himself to accept the answer he wanted to believe.

"I'm tired," Mom said, barely audibly. She had started slumping away from him, and Warren rose to right her. She obviously wanted to lie down, though, so he helped her slide back down to the pillow and he tucked the covers around her. Then he sat next to her on the bed, resting a hand on her shoulder, feeling the faint rise and fall of her breathing.

He looked across the bed. And though he couldn't see anything, he felt the soothing acknowledgment of gratefulness from a spirit that was definitely there with them. He nodded and then tilted his head back and closed his eyes, taking whatever remaining comfort he could from his mother's presence.

* * *

Will waited in the Camry, parked outside of the assisted living facility. The last couple of hours had been seriously crazy, to say the least. First Joseph had started getting weird on him after they stopped in the park. Then he'd managed to get weirder in the restaurant, saying strange things to the waitress about some food that only he could smell, then taking off for the kitchen, and showing up again at the front door.

As it turned out, that was the most rational part of the day. After that, Joseph was flat-out surreal, talking about knowing exactly where they needed to go and calling him Billy.

Then he dropped the big bomb. Joseph was Will's father. And, oh yeah, they were dead. According to Joseph, Will had been getting the wrong story from his foster parents all of this time. It wasn't that his parents had died, leaving him an orphan when he was only a toddler. It was that *he'd* died at that age and his fosters were serving as caretakers until his parents came to join him. According to Joseph, that was fifty-something years ago, though Will was only seventeen.

All of it was a bizarre jumble of facts that left Will feeling like he'd spent too much time on a carnival ride. Yet he knew it was true. He'd had an idea that he had some connection to Joseph from the moment he found the guy standing on the street across from his house. He'd had a strong desire to help Joseph instantly, and he'd found himself getting more and more caught up in Joseph's search the longer it went on. Several times, Will asked himself why he was taking this journey so personally. He liked Joseph and all, but his reaction went way beyond that. It was way out of proportion, but it still felt right.

Now he knew. Joseph wasn't the only one who'd been looking for home.

Their destination was only a short drive away which, considering where they were, made as much sense as anything else. Somehow, Will had the feeling that no matter where they were when the truth exploded on

Joseph, they would have only been a short drive from his wife. Excitement slowly replaced Will's sense of disorientation. He'd spent his entire life wondering about his parents. Then, all of a sudden, one was sitting next to him and they were going to meet the other.

Frustratingly, he couldn't go with Joseph into the assisted living place. He couldn't even get out of the car. It probably had something to do with this not being his world, but Will was just speculating. Would he get some kind of guidebook to the afterlife now that he was aware he was in it? He had an awful lot of questions.

It had been a long time since Joseph – should he be calling him Dad? Daddy? Father? Pop? – went inside. He could be waiting a while longer. Who knew how long a reunion like this lasted? He certainly hoped it was going well. Joseph would be a wreck if things didn't turn out okay.

He really had no choice but to wait, so he figured he might as well enjoy it. He put on the new Warren Zevon album, tilted back his seat slightly, and closed his eyes. He drifted along with the music, allowing his thoughts to settle. This had easily been the strangest week of his life, and it was going to take some time to figure everything out. He didn't have to figure it all out at once, though. He'd get to it – and he'd have help.

The album ended, he switched the music to random play, and he continued to wait. Patience had never been his greatest strength, but he was feeling pretty relaxed right now.

Maybe an hour or so later, he saw Joseph/Dad walking through the parking lot. Where his father had always seemed confused or at least intense during their five days together, he now appeared content and without a worry.

That probably had something to do with the beautiful woman in her early twenties whose arm was looped around his as they walked toward the car.

TWENTY-FIVE - Community Here

Warren grated lemon peel over the couscous and then sprinkled chopped parsley on top of that. Mom always served this dish with rice, but he was beginning to acknowledge that she opted for rice as her go-to starch far too often as it turned out. Tonight's meal was Don's Pucker-Up Fish. Dad loved acidic and briny flavors and Mom loaded them on in this dish. The sauce was a combination of lemon juice, lime juice, anchovies, capers, and salt-cured olives – a powerhouse of flavor that kept the taste buds on high alert for every bite. No one was complacent about eating this stuff.

Dad was definitely not complacent about it. He loved it, and Mom made it for him with great regularity. Warren, though, had always thought it was a bit over the top, though he'd never said as much to his mother. He decided to soften the acid content by adding fish stock and butter, and he cut back on the pungency by deleting the olives and anchovies. In their place, he grated some bottarga that he'd bought at a specialty store over the seared halibut after he sauced it. He'd eaten bottarga in Italian restaurants, but he'd had to call a half-dozen purveyors to find someone who carried it.

His mother had died three weeks ago today. She'd outlived her husband, her siblings, and several of her friends, so the funeral had had the potential to be a quiet affair. The people at Treetops had prevented that, though. A bus brought dozens of the residents, and many members of the staff came as well. Warren finally got to meet Keisha's brawny husband, and even found himself talking to the head cook, who turned out to have the soul of a foodie even though the facility's dietary restrictions had kept his talents out of the residents' dining room.

Jan was there, of course. She'd called him at home the night Mom died, after Warren had left Treetops and his mother's body had been taken away. He learned that Jan had left a message with each of the facility's shifts to inform her if anything happened to Antoinette. They stayed on the phone for forty-five minutes that night, as she allowed him to cry the tears he thought he'd already cried and to begin to understand how it was possible to feel shock and loss over something that he'd come to anticipate.

Two days later, when he came to bring home his mother's valuables (Treetops would donate whatever he didn't take), she helped him pack and then, in a shift from what had become their norm, took him out to lunch. They went to a Japanese restaurant, ate sushi – something his mother neither prepared nor liked – and shared stories. It was here that Warren learned that a man had been writing his mother love letters for most of the year before she began to sequester herself in her apartment. Mom had never mentioned the man or the letters, and Jan made it clear that the interest was entirely unidirectional. Warren felt a little bit of empathy for the man. He had no idea what he was up against when it came to Antoinette's affections.

After the funeral, Warren found himself suddenly alone. The bus had taken the residents back to Treetops, and the staff was gone, as were Warren's friends, relatives, and former colleagues. Crystal had come, which he appreciated, but she was gone now, too. Warren stood at the gravesite for several minutes, studying the tombstones of his father, mother, and brother standing together. It was something of a meditative experience, Warren allowing his mind to quiet, attempting to feel some sense of community with the three members of his family who had passed before him. It gave him a strong sense of peace, but a part of him quivered at the thought of being left behind.

However, when he turned, Jan was there, maybe twenty feet away. She pulled him into her arms and held him, letting him know that he had community here as well.

"Do you think you could come to dinner," he said when he finally stepped back from her embrace.

She smiled at him softly. "Do you really think you're up for cooking tonight?"

"Tonight? No, not tonight. Pizza, maybe. Or a big bag of Doritos. I was thinking maybe you could come for dinner, though. You know, the way you've been coming for lunch? I don't have the kitchen at Treetops anymore, so – "

Before he could finish the thought, she took him in her arms again and kissed him. In that moment, he set his sights on the future for the first time in more than a year. He held Jan's face in his hands and then kissed her again.

"I don't think I'm supposed to be feeling this way right now," he said.

Jan kissed his palm. "I think Antoinette would disagree with you."

Then she reached for him again.

He brought their fish into the dining area of his apartment, vowing once more to get a real table as soon as the money started coming in again. The folding table was fine when he was eating alone, especially since he took most of his meals on the couch anyway, but it just wouldn't do for Jan.

She'd poured wine and was already seated when he came in. "Pucker up," he said as he put the dish in front of her.

"If you insist," she said, pulling him toward her and offering him one of her soft, liquid kisses. Warren never failed to marvel at how Jan's kisses at once warmed and braced him. He thought he'd been finished with new romantic experiences as he headed toward forty, but he was thrilled to discover that he was utterly wrong.

"'Pucker Up' is the name of the fish," he said, kissing her again.

She gave him the kind of lascivious smile he'd never seen from her at Treetops. "I'm sure it is. Does that mean tomorrow you'll be making 'Lay Me Gently on the Carpet Stew?'"

"I can work with that," he said, his mind reeling, though not with cooking ideas.

She kissed him, and then reached around him for her fork. "The food is going to get cold."

"Did I mention that it was very tasty at room temperature?"

She gave him a playful push toward his chair. He watched her take her first bite and tilt her head toward him appreciatively, the only compliment he ever needed.

Warren took a forkful of couscous. "Danny called today. He wants me to start on Tuesday rather than Thursday next week. He's thinking two weeks of training and then he'll get me on the line."

Two weeks earlier, the son of one of the residents at Treetops had called Warren from out of the blue. He'd smelled Warren's cooking when he'd come to visit his father and had inquired of the staff why it stopped. When he learned that Warren's mother had died and that Warren was looking for work, he offered Warren the opportunity to become a line cook at one of his restaurants.

Warren's first reaction was that he was a corporate guy, not a restaurant guy. However, it only took another fifteen seconds of conversation for him to acknowledge that he'd never felt as much meaning from his work as he'd felt these past few months in the kitchen. His mother had always said that cooking for strangers would be different for her than cooking for relatives and friends. Warren was sure that he'd feel some of that difference, but not enough to make him reticent to pursue it.

"Oh, and I heard from the culinary academy. A new program starts in six weeks."

"So you're going to do it?"

"Danny said he'll work with me. He thinks cooking school is a great idea. He hinted that it was going to be essential if I were ever to graduate from chopping vegetables in one of his kitchens."

Jan took his hand and brought it to her lips. "Quite the whirlwind, huh?"

Warren sat back in his chair, trying to absorb it all. He had a new career and a new mission. Most importantly, he had a woman in his life who'd given him the most soul-stirring reason to come home he'd ever had.

The thought made him laugh out loud.

Don wanted the Pucker-Up Fish again. She'd made it for him the second day here, but he was so persuasive, and she'd never been able to deny him anything, especially when it came to food. She hoped she didn't bore the others. They were going to have an eternity of meals together. If they had to have the same thing every couple of weeks, they might get a little tired of it.

The first few days here had her head spinning. Reuniting with her sisters Maggie and Rachel, her sister-in-law

Carmela, her brother-in-law Sal, her dear neighbor Ralph, and all the others in that oversized house they all shared. Getting accustomed to her new body, which was really a version of her old body from decades ago. It seemed that when you were here you became an age you particularly loved. Antoinette had started in her early twenties, but Don was in his early forties and the age difference was a bit awkward, even under the circumstances. By the time they'd gone to bed that first night, though, she'd moved up to her late twenties and he'd come down to his mid-thirties. Of course, when they got into bed that night, they were ageless. Time meant nothing when they were wrapped together. It had always been that way and Antoinette knew it would always continue to be that way.

Antoinette still had faint memories of the body she'd left behind, the one that failed to respond to her commands and that housed a mind that had lost its keenness. Those memories were fading, though. It was difficult to hold on to such thoughts when you felt as spry and sharp as she felt.

She finished putting the fish on a platter and spooning sauce over it. There would be fourteen for dinner tonight. There had never been less than eight and there had been as many as twenty-four when they invited others from the neighborhood. It turned out that, unlike Billy, everyone else in the house had known exactly where they were all along. They could have explained as much to Don when he got there, but they knew even before he woke up that he had to come back for her before he could ever settle. Antoinette and Carmela took turns making the main dishes, with the other providing the sides. Carmela had tended to be a little competitive with her in the past, but here she was very generous. Perhaps that was one of the additional blessings of this place.

The others were in the middle of some kind of boisterous conversation when Antoinette came out of the kitchen. She brought the platter over to Don and Billy to allow them to serve themselves first before putting the rest on the table. This generated jovial protests of favoritism from the others, but Antoinette just smiled and acknowledged that she was very definitely playing favorites.

She sat between her husband and son. Don immediately gave her the comical fish-face kiss he always offered when she made this dish for him. Billy kissed her lightly on the cheek.

"I didn't know food could taste like this, Mom."

"You *did*," Antoinette said. "You just forgot."

Billy took another huge bite of the fish before loading his plate with Carmela's potatoes and vegetables. "I'm glad I'm remembering now. I can't believe what I've been missing. Are you going to be naming more dishes after me?"

Two nights before, Antoinette had created her first new meal since she got here. She called it "Billy's All-My-Tomorrows Pork Chops." The day she came home from the hospital after her baby had died, she'd seen a bowl of rotten pears she'd planned to cook and puree for him before he got sick and their world turned upside down. He'd always loved pureed pears. For the first dish she ever named for her first son, she sautéed pears in butter, finished them with a little brown sugar and brandy, and served them over grilled pork chops. Billy ate three chops and she could swear that the smile he wore when he took his first bite was the same smile he'd worn when he'd played in his high chair while she cooked. She had to excuse herself for a moment after that.

"I'm working on a new idea now," she said.

Billy gave her another of his grins and then concentrated on his food. Antoinette caught up with the conversation around the table, something about a new department store that had popped up downtown overnight. The magic of this place continued to dazzle her. Billy was taking Don and her on a car ride tomorrow to explore more of it. There was so much to discover. And so much to embrace.

Antoinette prayed that Warren was doing well. As her clarity of mind returned, she realized what the last year of her life had been like. Warren had been unbelievably good to her and she'd made things so much harder for him than she would have wanted. She loved that he tried to cook for her. Antoinette also found it fascinating that he'd taken to cooking for the nurse, Jan – a very pretty, very nice woman – when she could no longer eat. Antoinette had overheard their conversations, though she couldn't comment on them. They seemed to have quite a spark, though it wasn't obvious whether Warren noticed this. He'd never been the best with women. Something told her Warren was going to get it right this time, though.

Some day, he'd grace this table. Maybe both of them would. Not for a long time, though, she hoped. They had so much more of their journey left before they came home.

A Note To My Readers

Each of my novels has had a strong source of inspiration. This has never been truer than with *The Journey Home*. My parents' marriage was always something that dazzled me. They made up a seamless whole together. They entertained and regaled one another, supported one another through tragedy, and always seemed to want to be together. It was simply impossible to think of one without the other. My father was the only man my mother ever dated and she proclaimed this proudly. My father actually had a thing for my mother's sister before he met my mother. My aunt showed absolutely no interest in his affections, which my father considered the luckiest break of his life, as it led him to her very cute younger sibling.

When my father died, the emptiness my mother felt was un-fillable. As Antoinette does in this novel, she went to an assisted living facility where she found entertainment and companionship (along with all the tasteless butter cookies she could eat). However, she never spent a day after my father died when she didn't wish she could be with him instead. As Alzheimer's took its toll, she still spoke about him with clarity. And when she got very sick toward the end of her life, she told my sisters and me about conversations she was having with my dad where he told her he was waiting for her. We all knew exactly where those conversations were leading. They struck me when my mother first told me about them and they led me to write *The Journey Home*.

About the Author

Lou Aronica is the coauthor of the *New York Times* best-sellers *The Element* and *Finding Your Element* (both with Sir Ken Robinson) and the national bestseller *The Culture Code* (with Clotaire Rapaille) and the author of the *USA Today* bestselling novel *The Forever Year* and the national bestselling novels *Blue, When You Went Away, The Journey Home* and *Leaves*, among others. He lives in Southern Connecticut with his wife and four children. A long-term book industry veteran, he is the President and Publisher of the independent publishing house The Story Plant and a past president of Novelists Inc.

You can reach Lou at laronica@fictionstudio.com.